THE EVERYTHING CELL

Fred Penn

Note to the reader
This book has a theme of suicidal ideation

CONTENTS

NOWHERE

"What's the most important question that could be asked?"

"None I've asked already? Then tell me."

"If asking questions is most important, then the answer is the same question: 'What's the most important question that could be asked?' So the most important inquiry of all would end before starting. Don't place so much value in your questions."

"Well, perhaps I don't... but in answers."

"Experience is a constant stream of answers, ending only with you."

1   MIDDLE

where am I, what am I doing here

Numb light flooded a brain, and from within a curled ball of fresh sheets, a man had jolted upright in bed.

Morning, entering through a walled opening above, filled a clinical white space. Instinctively, the man left the bed's solid structure and stood up, with strong yet undefined intentions, when a new and unfamiliar question struck.

who *am I*

Something uncanny revealed itself. As if winded, the man collapsed back onto the soft bedding, where he proceeded to sit motionless. His fallen gaze was gradually absorbed by a canvas-like floor.

On the floor's surface, faint formless shadows weaved in and out of existence, and in a trance, the man followed their dance. Behind the movements were quiet strips of vertical shadow spaced out evenly. Becoming more pronounced as the light changed, these static columns now attracted his notice.

Turning, he was greeted by sunlight splitting through a neatly barred window. He stepped up. Barefooted on the bed, he peered out. The air felt fresher, and he imagined nearby pine forests. Yet facing him, a few feet away and forming one side of a cuboid alcove, was just a pale-grey concrete wall. At the top of the wall there'd be blue sky, but he couldn't angle his head to see that far up. Rather than blue, grey only gave way to more grey, which did the same.

He turned his back on the window. In the far corner to his right was the outline of a white door on one of the white walls. He walked over. There was no handle, so he pressed his hands into the large upright rectangle. Nothing happened. He knocked on it quietly, but again with no result. Giving himself a second try, he rapped on it.

nothing

The man traced his steps back to the window.

The problem was the bars. Despite how he repositioned himself, their flat line constantly obstructed his view. In invisible increments, his frustration increased; residue anger loosened and mixed in. The man burst out.

Enraged, he hit the steel line with his palms and forearms. Cursing, he pulled at a bar, determined to yank it out. He thumped it. He had an angry urge for freedom.

I've woken up to I don't even know what and I'm trapped!

Dismissing the window, he thudded off the bed and marched back across to the door, abuse for it already leaping ahead. He crashed into white steel, kicking and thumping. He was yelling: making requests, demands, threats and finally abuse – each utterance a torn fragment from the savage race to get out. Yet all he had was engulfed effortlessly by a shapeless silence.

He slumped down against the flat metal of his opponent, arms bruised and toes stubbed. Chin landed on chest – his throat was hoarse and he wanted to cry. Holding his head, he massaged closed eyes and straightened up. He steadied his breathing. Although not calm, he'd spent his rage. He confronted his new and yet only world for the first time soberly.

Its whiteness consisted of smart planes of paint covering the walls, door, floor and ceiling. The floor and door, from underneath and behind, met his flesh-and-bone body with ungiving hardness. He knocked on the wall. The entire room was made of thick steel: it was this that surrounded him beneath the veneer. He pondered on the fact but it wasn't productive, imagining chipping a tooth on the hard floor.

Getting to his feet, his attention was caught by a gleam to his left. It came from a small metallic dome. The dome was placed on a small pure-white table at the foot of the bed. Hungry, he was sure it contained food. With the white table was a white chair, both cold-and-hard-looking.

As he walked over, the line of bars at the window taunted him about the world beyond.

no, I at least need a break first

He was hungry. Raising the domed lid from the table, warm steam burst out, carrying beef and potato up into his nostrils. There were rich-green vegetables too. Pulling up the chair, he sat down to eat. The food was satisfying and he was soon finished.

Savouring the taste of a good meal, the man stood leaning against the door-hosting wall. With eyes running free along its smooth expanse to his left, he felt much-needed new energy. Jutting out at waist height was a small piece of non-white shiny plumbing, beyond which were the table and chair where he'd just eaten.

Bringing his head back, he turned his attention to the wall opposite. Fixed at its centre was a large non-white toilet made of plain thick steel. He walked over to its left and gave it a sharp tap with the outer bony edge of his foot. The precision of the dull ache and sound was pleasurable. Across the toilet's basin was a flat steel sheet which looked like it might retract. He wondered if he should find this odd. Turning back, he proceeded to pace back and forth across the cell. His meal walked off a little, he stopped in the centre, before venturing back to the toilet where he took a seat.

Looking over to the corner where he'd just eaten, the man realised he was thirsty. No drink had been supplied with the meal. He looked again at the piece of non-white plumbing which jutted out of the wall, though now from a new angle. Across from him, a steel chunk of rectangle protruded horizontally like a tray. On its front left corner was a thick cylinder which stood up like a periscope. Already he'd begun to hope it was a drinking fountain.

He crossed the cell, his eyes on the head of the periscope.

that must be where the water jets out

Crouched down, he examined the inner side. At its top was a hole through which water might flow. Casting his eyes onto the tray, its surface was marked with small holes through which excess water might pass.

it must *be a fountain*

His hands and eyes groped to work it, and then a cold burst of water splashed his cheek. It felt clean. He looked to check this before angling his mouth to gulp down the clear, fluid line. After he'd had enough, it stopped.

He walked over to the bed, stretched out, and looked at the white ceiling above. He was satisfied physically. The man part-rolled onto his left side and looked around the strange room. He knew he was being detained in a cell, but that much was obvious and the questions remained.

I still don't know where I am or why I'm here

He was again disturbed by the most haunting inscrutability of all.

I don't even know who *I am… I know I'm a human*

being… there must be an important reason for all this

He reigned in scattered thoughts.

I've already fought with my surroundings and made a clamour and it's got me nowhere

The pain in his bruised hands and feet started to ripen.

no one's come… but I've been given food and water… it seems fairly certain that someone will come soon, meanwhile patience is best by default… but what about my memories, they won't come walking through the door, if I can just briefly remember what happened before…

The man groaned for an absent past.

However, his despairing mood didn't last long. He was determined to regain his memory and so set about the attempt. He encountered a mind blurred, like an unfinished oil painting abandoned in a storm. He shuddered: perhaps forever ruined or erased, his memories might never return. Hope flashed.

at least my mind isn't just a clean slate, there must be elements of real in it

His imaginings had to be based on something. But his confidence deflated before he could secure it.

of course the fundamental elements are real… colours shapes emotions body parts… it's whether I'm able to put them back together so they resemble my past… structure… how can I know my memories are real

Roaming the mind, the question sought to undermine his mission. His imagination became increasingly prone to mutation, and he was forced to stop.

Resettling uncomfortably on the decision to wait for someone, emotional exhaustion struck. He turned onto his front. Cheek buried in pillow, he submitted to the beginnings of an unnatural sleep, when from somewhere on a dream's verge, a name came to him. No sooner was the name in his head, his tongue threw it out: "Cameron". He repeated it more loudly. Hearing the sound fill the cell's empty surroundings, the man recognised it as his own name.

that's me that's my name!

"Cameron!"

Excitement roused him awake. Although only a sound, it carried an identity. He could attach things to it. More importantly, the man now had a reason to believe his memory would return.

I know my name and I didn't before, that's significant… and got by none other than the power of my own memory!

2   COMMUTE

A man was underground waiting for a train, and his name was Cameron.

He was stood in a large horizontal corridor, which a train platform cut across perpendicularly to his left. His back was to a wall and facing him was an abstract artwork.

The work was a grey pencil-and-paint grid of small vertical rectangles drawn on a square white canvas. Cameron's eyes strayed to the grid's boundaries. It wasn't boxed in, rather incomplete at the edges where the lines struck nothing: a square fragment of a rectangular pattern which went on indefinitely. His mind followed the pattern's expansion. He followed it out of the four sides of the frame simultaneously, on and on in all directions. He then viewed the pattern coming off the canvas, and continuing both towards and away from him.

Looking to his left, he saw people were starting to crowd onto the platform. They were forming an orderly row, lining the track in expectation of the train. There was a risk he might not be able to get on the next one; already a second row was forming in his field of vision. However, he didn't want to queue with the others. Besides this, he was appreciating the art before him, which was in fact the reason he was here. He'd stay where he was, and, when the train appeared on his left, he'd get on. He leaned more weight back onto the cooling wall behind.

With the artwork still there, he wondered whether he liked it and waited for an answer to come. There was a mathematical neatness about it which produced elegance. Still, there was almost nothing there. It certainly was mathematical: a section of graph paper, only with a rectangular instead of square pattern. Curiously, Martin had always denied his work was minimalist. In any case, the Government liked such art.

Staring into the mathematical spaces, Cameron started to quarter them, smaller and smaller, using the same pattern which created them. He was lost in the eternal again but then halted, amused at what masqueraded as an infinitely small rectangle. He cut it up, proving it wrong, only to be left with four new challengers in its place.

Cameron felt a smooth, powerful noise charging through a tunnel, and realised his train was fast approaching. He cast a glance at the other commuters: patiently lined along the platform edge as tons of metal careered towards them. The rumble would bring the train to quickly fill up what was before his left.

The train had appeared and was slowing down. He refused the idea of waiting for another one, deciding he had to get on. He darted across the platform. Pushing through a thin point in the lines, he found himself relieved to be in a quiet carriage.

Although he'd carried in some reproving looks, he'd be off at the next stop as he needed to change lines.

Earlier that morning, Cameron had eaten his usual breakfast. It was a nutritious set meal. He'd had it back in his ground-floor apartment with his wife, who ate one of the smaller-portioned female options. Later outside, he'd kissed her on the cheek, momentarily feeling the rush it still gave them both, before they commenced their separate working lives.

Today was slightly different though. As was their habit, they'd got up early and had breakfast together. However, usually, Cameron would use the extra time this then gave him to walk to work, leaving earlier than his wife, the two parting at the front door. His wife used her extra morning time to sketch. In fact, it was due to her artistic streak that today, leaving the apartment together, they'd parted later at the courtyard gardens, and altering his routine, Cameron was taking the train.

Martin, his wife's friend, had won a competition to make the capital's train network his underground gallery. Owing to his wife, officially Martin was Cameron's friend too. So, when she excitedly told him the news, Cameron was obliged to visit the art.

Even once approved and installed, Cameron had postponed going to see Martin's work on display. It wasn't that he disliked Martin or his art. Despite having little in common, he'd always liked Martin and was curious to see what he'd created. However, he also liked his morning walk and routine.

As well as this, he disliked the underground trains. It was this he'd tried to explain to his wife unsuccessfully before. Here had come another occasion which demanded the attempt. The problem was that he didn't fully understand the aversion himself. Sometimes Cameron wished he lived in a smaller city where people walked or cycled, or perhaps somewhere rural.

Arriving on foot at the next platform for his connection, Cameron was relieved to see the train waiting for him this time. He rushed towards it to jump on. It was emptier than the first, and he found a seat as the train accelerated.

Resting back, he briefly studied the man sitting opposite. He had jet-black hair, slightly combed over, and was reading a newspaper. He was a tall, well-built man who looked in his late thirties. Cameron was idly gazing at a crease in his forehead when the strong eyes beneath returned his look. There was jarring eye contact and Cameron instinctively flicked his pupils away. A bit stressed and tired, without fully realising, Cameron's eyes soon settled on the same face there before him. He watched the features, and his doing so caused the man to lose concentration on his paper, the forehead tensing slightly. The man was aware Cameron was looking at him again, but he was pretending not to notice.

Cameron had no special interest in this fellow stranger. He got up, turned his back on the man and faced the doors, waiting to get off.

3   GUARD

The man lay on his bed in elated relief. How much time had elapsed since he'd first said his name, he didn't know.

such good progress already and this is just the start

He felt detached from the person in the memory, but this wasn't something to dwell on.

I'm already starting to feel myself again… and how about that self, I have a wife, maybe even a family, perhaps I'll be released soon, maybe today when the guard comes, and then I can go back to my comfortable apartment to be with them and my life will come flooding back around me

The memory had stopped just as he was getting off the train and he wanted to learn more about his life; he still didn't really understand who he was. However, he needed respite after the wave of information which had just crashed on him. He wasn't given any rest at present.

Echoes of activity from the other side of the door wandered into the cell. Intent on catching them, the man stood up and moved into the centre. The flat white door was about to open. He took an anxious step forwards but then rushed back, impulsively deciding to be found seated on the bed.

The steel door opened inwards. On its other side, evidently, its hinges were unconventionally fixed on the edge furthest from the corner in which it stood in the cell. As the white rectangle silently pivoted towards the direction of the bed, the man was only offered a slightly fuller view of it, rather than an opportunity of glimpsing outside.

The door had barely moved when a woman entered wearing a plain cyan uniform. Having appeared, she calmly turned her back on the surroundings. She placed safely in her pocket a set of keys she'd been holding. Pushing the steel door into the identically white wall, she pressed it to make sure it was sealed shut.

The woman looked young. However, once she'd turned back and they were looking at each other, she became ageless. The clear forehead stood above modest planar cheeks formed at high angles. Yet behind the steady brown eyes, the man met someone who was intimate with time. He suddenly felt nervous in her presence, and a little ridiculous at having first advanced before retreating back to receive her. She smiled, and kindness imbued the once unreadable face.

"Hello. I expect you have lots of questions." "Yes," the man said excitedly, taking the opportunity to stand up. "Well, all in good time. Rest assured, we want you out of here as quickly as possible." The age of her voice agreed with her appearance. "Good," he replied, feeling a little stupid at his response, though at a loss to make any other. She had stated things so clearly and without any prompting, he felt he'd come across as somehow immature if he proceeded with his questions now. Now there was someone before him ready to ask, the exact meanings and forms of the questions became furtive.

He was about to sit down again but caught himself, conscious he'd only just stood up. "It's getting late though," continued the woman, nodding to the window. Outside dusk had long arrived. Glancing up, the man noticed a light had come on in the cell. "You must be hungry. I'll get you your dinner. Sorry, you should've been given it earlier." She walked over to the table and collected the cutlery from lunch. Deftly unlocking the door, she left, and the white rectangle closed shut behind her.

Soon back, she had a new plate of food which she placed on the table, while the man stood awkwardly by. She returned to the door, rotated and fixed her eyes on him. The way she was stood, or poised, she appeared both stationed on duty yet also about to leave.

"Thank you," he remembered. "Lucy," replied the woman. "My name's Lucy," she explained. The mutual space shifted as she approached him with an outstretched hand. "I'm Cameron," the man replied, shaking hands. As she took his hand, he realised she was taller. "Cameron," the woman repeated back to him. It sounded like a question at first. However, the responsive smile and assertive gaze explained she was simply being attentive to the introduction. "Lucy," he offered back in exchange.

"OK then, I'll be going now. Enjoy your dinner, Cameron. Today's is fish pie. I imagine after you'll be wanting an early night – no doubt it's been a long day. Good night." "Wait," he called out. She turned back from the door and looked at him. "We can talk more tomorrow, OK? Let's talk then, in the morning," she told him. He was alone again.

4 GRENADE

"Please be patient," Cameron was told when his questions finally met Lucy. On his pressing further, she'd assured him that the procedure for his removal from the cell was already underway and things would become clearer very soon. Meanwhile, he'd be looked after. Meanwhile, Cameron was bored.

He often poured over his one memory privately. In practical terms, the primary function of this was an antidote to the boredom, though Cameron avoided ever admitting this explicitly. Nonetheless, it also brought him closer to his mysterious self, which currently he felt was all he really had, giving a loosely recognisable shape to reality. He tried to use the memory's contents to deduce more. Simultaneously, however, he was wary of inculcating the thought that he'd already been granted enough. He didn't want to become too settled with the memory and so deter any potential new ones.

As well as his memory, Cameron also thought about Lucy, though caution warned him not to introduce each to the other, at least for the time being. Despite Cameron feeling like a lone soldier in his dreary combat with monotony, Lucy supported him in his campaign. She stopped by often, not just at mealtimes. She was a pleasing conversationalist, guiding them through a seamless expanse of shifting topics as they talked away. On one occasion, just before hearing the door open, Cameron had decided to consciously follow her distinctively subtle art and hence learn from her. In a single lapse, the project was discarded in favour of unreflective interaction. Based on his recollections, he and Lucy never talked about much in particular. Perhaps it was this he enjoyed most. However, on certain recent visits, Lucy's behaviour had given him plenty to think about.

The first of such visits happened one fresh mid-morning, when the sun and air outside were both of their time of day. Just as the first time Cameron encountered Lucy some days before, the blank rectangle of door contained her complete attention as she entered the cell. So far this was all normal. As had become customary, next she would have turned from the shut door and warmly greeted him, conversation ensuing.

On this occasion, turning around, Lucy immediately directed Cameron's attention towards the bed. "What is it?" she asked, as though testing him. Slightly vexed, he answered uncertainly, "It's a bed." He guarded himself with a half-serious tone and the beginnings of a quizzical look. Standing exactly as before, Lucy reappeared before him in her smooth blue-green clothing but this time with a clipboard and pen.

She joined him at the centre of the cell and looked up from the board at his slowly rising eyebrows. Focusing on his eyes, now housed by the two furry shallow arches, she addressed his expression, "I just need to ask a few simple questions." Daylight entering through the window irradiated her features. "I'm certain you'll have no trouble with them, but I need to follow procedure all the same." With unmasked benevolence, she added, "And I know you'll be pleased to hear, Cameron, that it's all part of the very same procedure to get you out of here." Realising, though in an unexpected guise, this turn of events was part of what he'd been waiting for, Cameron was indeed pleased to hear this. His vexation dissipated, "Great! Well let's get this done then!"

Resuming, Lucy directed his attention again towards the bed, this time asking for a description. She emphasised that he should be brief and just describe it as it appeared to him. Next, the bed's purpose was requested. This seemed a strange concept. After some thought, Cameron gave the answer his best attempt, "It's somewhere for people to sleep… it helps people sleep." "Good, I knew you'd do fine," Lucy replied, "And the last of the four: How is it used?" This one was easier, "Well, you lie on it and sleep…" "… Anything else?" she asked, encouragingly. There was a pause as he considered. "Most people have some of the sheets over them I suppose…. and your head goes on the pillow." "Excellent." With that Lucy proceeded, directing Cameron's attention from the bed to the floor and executing the same line of inquiry: name; physical description; purpose; method of use.

So it was that such visits ensued. They were always at irregular times. In one instance, it was some indistinct phase of night when Lucy came: with the clipboard held in one hand, she'd gently woken up Cameron with the other. They'd gone through the questions in relative dark. It was soon over, and Cameron was allowed to slump back into sleep. In all cases, as soon as she arrived, she went straight to it, asking Cameron to identify various things around the cell. She always asked the same set series of questions: "What is it?" "Describe it." "Purpose?" "How is it used?"

Although at first Cameron had been unclear what was required of him, he apparently supplied satisfactory answers all the same, though granted often not succinctly. Becoming more familiar with and well-practised at the exercise, he could rattle off the set of four answers on prompting. After a particularly long session, his brain started successions of answers automatically, often interrupted and restarted, in accordance with his shifting attention from object to object. He never rattled off the answers to Lucy though; following protocol, he waited patiently for each question to be repeated in turn.

An unusually long gap of two whole days had now passed since Lucy's last official visit as tester. After she'd brought Cameron his dinner, he'd asked her if the testing was over. She'd said she wasn't disposed to say, though then swept both her arms out, seeming to envelop everything in the cell. Combined with her expression, it suggested that he'd now surely been asked the questions for every individual thing there. In some cases, he'd even been asked the questions for things which acted as the elementary components of other things.

It was in bed from where Cameron thought on all this. His head rested on his pillow. From there, in the dimming light, his eyes peered around his cell. He now knew it so well and realised he'd partly be sad to leave. Accompanied by a strangely satisfying pride, he waited for sleep.

He was next aware that on the other side of his eyelids daylight was beckoning. He'd woken up peacefully inside first, not from an external barrage on the senses. His muscles seemed in a similar position before dreaming, and it felt like he'd barely moved all night. A long wave of restfulness slowly rolled through his bones. He took physical pleasure in the simple act of not moving, save for the odd stretch.

After a while, it was time to move properly. He started slowly, with the opening of the eyes. The bright light, striking the two small watery surfaces, was pleasurably painful. Breaking his eyes' embrace with the shaded linen closest, Cameron took in the lit-up ocean of whiteness that was his floor.

On doing so, he immediately discovered that a small black island had appeared at its centre. Still adjusting, his pupils each drank in the light awkwardly like newborns. Together finding focus, they confirmed that the black spot was real: not contained within warm blinks but sat out on the white metal floor. It appeared something new had arrived, placed at the centre of his small world.

Cameron sat upright, wide awake, the bare soles of his feet planted on the cool steel beneath. Before him was the strange black object. He was leaning forwards slightly, staring across at it. He was about to stand up and walk over for a closer look.

The door opened and in came Lucy. Cameron's muscles willingly disregarded their orders to stand. He leaned back, relaxing into shoulder blades, with hands splayed out behind him on the soft bed. He gazed over at Lucy.

is this the first time I'm seeing her a little rushed

She had her usual composure, as she placed the keys in her pocket and faced the door to press it shut. However, unlike other times, her attention seemed slightly divided: focused not just on the door and her present actions, but also on the cell behind her in the adjacent future.

On turning to face the cell, she marched over to the small black object. Once there, she appeared to relax. She crouched down beside the object and beckoned Cameron over. As he brought his weight forwards and up from the bed, she took out the familiar clipboard and pen. Cameron walked over to the collection of Lucy, the clipboard, the pen and the small black object.

"What is it?" Lucy asked. "I don't know," replied Cameron, "I've just woken up and seen it here this morning." He fixed his eyes on hers as he said this. He'd just glanced at the object as he'd crouched down, and recognised that he perhaps didn't want to know what it was after all. "Well, have a look," she prompted, reflecting back a smile, "and see if you can tell me."

On the white floor before him was the resemblance of a giant rotten-black kiwi. However, not soft and fuzzy, its surface was hard and notched. He reluctantly balanced what he saw in his mind.

The object looked of a size, heaviness and temperature satisfying to hold and weigh in the palm. He felt he wasn't allowed to touch it, nor was he eager. At what might be called its top, facing away from him, was a large ring pull, thinly framing a generous disc of air. Unlike the main body, which was pure black, this part was a dangerous bright red and at first looked alien to the rest of the object.

A single word arrived to crystallise Cameron's foggy notions.

grenade

"It's a grenade," he answered, caught slightly by the apparent naturalness of his own voice. "Good, you see, you do know," chimed in Lucy. "Next – please describe it." "It's small, black and the shape of a kiwi. But perhaps three times the size. It looks hard, cold and weighty. There's a red metal ring attached to it." "What's its purpose?" There was a short silence. "It kills people... blows them and other things up." Lucy was immersed in her clipboard as she busily made notes to this. She never halted in proceeding with the set of questions. At the end of each answer, she started the next question, and presently came the final one: "How is it used?" "You pull the ring away from the main body, detaching it, and then throw the body at whatever it is you want to blow up." "Precisely right," Lucy answered, impressed, "or at whatever it is you want to gas," she added to herself, "depending what type of grenade you have."

She completed her notes, and then looked up and onto Cameron's face. "A variety of grenades exist," she began in a lecturing tone, "Anti-personnel fragmentation grenades kill or damage their target by a dispersal of lethal fragments upon detonation. These fragments partly consist of the grenade's body, made of a hard synthetic material or steel, and explode off as shards or splinters." She paused and gave the grenade, lying on the floor before her audience, a gentle but resounding knock with the central knuckle of her middle finger.

She looked back at his face now lost, but unfazed continued, "Now, *concussion* grenades are so called because it's the concussion effect, rather than the shards and splinters, which guarantees death." She picked up the black object, and delicately handling it went on, "There's more explosive filler in these grenades and the case is thinner. They're offensive grenades and the effective killing zone is relatively small." She looked around the cell. "But they shake the sky like thunder nevertheless!" Enthralled at her own words, Lucy looked up at the ceiling, seemingly peering through as if in a poetic trance.

All the while, Cameron was utterly vexed at this impromptu show-and-tell lecture. He was especially confused by how he was expected to respond. The situation surely wasn't a normal one. Lucy's behaviour, as the only other participant, asserted it wasn't so strange after all. Lecturing came very naturally to her. There wasn't a single subject on which he wouldn't have been surprised next to find out she was also an apparent expert.

Lucy's lecture exhibit was still supply gripped in her hand. Carrying it into the air, she drew his attention closer, "You see it has a notched surface – a notched surface aids fragmentation." "So this isn't the concussion grenade?" Cameron asked out loud, "This is the type that kills you by exploding splinters and shards?" he added, mild concern and repulsion mixing coarsely in his voice. "Ah, well actually it's a notched surface on the *inside* that improves fragmentation," replied Lucy, pleased to have an attentive pupil. "It turns out that a notched surface on the outside doesn't help. But the design's been retained as it provides better grip. And it does look better, don't you agree?" she added, with an inviting beam. "So which type is this one then? How does it kill you?" Cameron witnessed her distracted, perhaps disappointed at the opportunity for shared aesthetic appreciation passing by untouched. Before a complete moment though, she was lecturer again. "*Both* types typically have this notched surface you can see here," she explained informatively, carefully placing their attention back on the grenade and running her slender fingers over its surface.

"But," she went on with a change of tone, "most important is that you know that this is a real working grenade here." She held it up again. As they looked at each other, it parted their mutual channels of vision. "If you pulled this ring off," she said, touching it gently with a graceful index finger, "– and it comes off quite easily with a little force – then it would set the grenade off in the cell, and your death would swiftly and inevitably follow." She explained this warningly. Cameron was about to say something, but Lucy had now arrived at her own question with more momentum. "Do you understand?" she asked, in a smoothly concluding tone. "Yes", answered Cameron, "but—"

But Lucy was now talking to her clipboard. "OK, that's very reassuring to know," she rolled on, ticking a box as she said this. Then suddenly remembering with a female voice, "You must be hungry! It's late already and I still haven't got you your breakfast!" She was already almost at the door, "Today we're having boiled eggs and toast." The door was open, "I'll be back in a moment with the food." She was gone.

* * *

Lucy was soon back with breakfast. Cameron was sitting in a daze on the bed, unwillingly absorbed by the new object before him. "Come on," she roused him. "You can think about that later if you must. Come and eat," she said cheerfully. He wanted to say something to her about the grenade, before she was whisked away again to leave him with his breakfast, but at present he couldn't form any material with which to speak.

Lucy's current flyby visit was already partway through and headed for completion. She'd talked away in her habitual manner as she'd carried out her duties. Now she was gone again.

She left Cameron standing by the table, looking down at his food. He sat down. He wasn't hungry. As usual, fruit was part of breakfast. Cameron felt slightly nauseous as he looked into a pomegranate cut in two: the glistening beads, delicately packed in the fleshy skin, seemed ready to explode. "Hmm." He pushed the bowl of fruit away but resolved to make an effort on the two boiled eggs. He mechanically ate a little at a time, in the end managing about half of each.

Staying sat at the table, he was thinking.

today is not a normal day… I know it… that morning lecture wasn't, and why a morning lecture in the first place anyway

He looked behind him to be reminded of the grenade's presence.

what's it still doing *here*

From afar, then in a flash in focus and upon him, the fuller question smacked him flush.

why have I been left alone with a grenade in my cell! a real *working grenade!*

He felt something like heat rise within him. His insides constricted as if in anticipation, wanting to trap and keep it down. He didn't recognise it for indignation.

it just doesn't make any sense, this isn't how prisons are supposed to be… a mistake must've been made… Lucy's something of an eccentric in her own subtle ways, she isn't your usual guard, she must've forgotten it… it's her *grenade, maybe it's part of some enigmatic collection and she must've forgotten it… she'll take it away in a short while… at lunch when she collects my things from breakfast*

Refusing to admit he wasn't completely satisfied with this reasoning, yet not in the mood to think on it any more, Cameron crossed the short distance of floor from his chair at the table to his bed. He lay back and looked up at the ceiling. He felt restless.

I'll make sure Lucy remembers to take her grenade back away with her next time… at lunch

Increate thoughts were near and he blindly shooed them away.

no, it's the best and only thing I can do, there's nothing else to do now besides worry, and there's no use in that… I don't want a grenade, that's for sure… what's there to do with it, besides kill people, I don't want that… and it's dangerous, having a thing like that lying around in a confined space like this… yes, I can explain all that to Lucy, or wait no I won't have to, she's probably just forgotten it… but if I do need to I can explain

He stole a glance at the grenade to his left and waited for Lucy impatiently.

Lucy returned to exchange breakfast's old cutlery for lunch. A loquacious breeze, she was already on her way back to the door to leave. She hadn't paid any attention to the grenade, nor given Cameron a chance to on her behalf.

He had no choice but to interrupt. He tried to do so politely, "You've forgotten the grenade." "What's that?" she threw back. He'd mumbled a little and so repeated his statement, but Lucy only seemed to hear the last word. She was all too happy to take him up on the topic. Cameron received his second talk of the day on grenades.

She had a toolbox of terms: 'safety levers', 'strikers', 'rotations', 'detonation', 'primers', 'fuses', 'delay elements', 'main charges'. He'd distractedly paid attention when it was commented that the grenade in his cell didn't have a safety lever. However, this aside, he didn't follow any of what was said: he was groping for somewhere to pierce through her loose fabric of conversation.

To his dismay, the same situation was repeating its natural course, despite his new resolution to catch her. Although reserved a main role in the scene, his own will simply didn't factor in. She was again at the door.

Distress at his own helplessness and inadequacy took hold. Lucy didn't notice as she talked herself away. The door was open and she was on the verge of abandoning him. Urgency caught his stomach in a pincer, and he cried out, "Wait! You've forgotten your grenade! Please, I don't want it in my cell. Could you take it away with my breakfast things? Here, I'll put it on the tray for you." He spoke loudly and clearly, not shouting but still resorting to vocal force to get his words in.

He turned and made to collect the grenade, in order to give it to Lucy as he'd suggested. Lucy's voluminous conversation vanished from the cell. Cameron halted, a sudden silence threatening him. Now he wished her current of talk would restart. Compelled, he turned back to face her.

As they made eye contact, Lucy's expression assured him that she knew he wasn't being confrontational. Cameron felt relieved. "It's not my

grenade," she explained, "So it's not mine to take."
Continuing with a lighter tone, "But what's wrong
with it being in here anyway? You've got enough
space. Please, enjoy the lunch. Perhaps get some rest
too – you look like you didn't sleep well last night.
I'll be back later with your dinner. See you then." She
quietly slipped out.

5   TRANSLUCENT MEETING

"I've some exciting news," announced a commanding voice. Cameron was in a meeting. He was seated in a quiet, comfortable room with about fifteen other people. Stretched out before him was dark polished mahogany. It was the surface of the table around which they were all sitting. To his right was the dark-grey suit sleeve and shoulder belonging to the person next to him. Looking up and passed this, his eyes met with the voice's source.

It belonged to the only person in the room standing, and everyone else gave him their full attention. His hair was fair, and he had a slim build. Apart from this, he looked a little like the man Cameron remembered seeing on the train, only his eyes were also different. Ablaze with lustreless grey, they were large, round and vacant. Yet he had the countenance of an active leader, in accord with his posture. This was the Director General of Law.

"As we all know, our law computer program has been an excellent success." There was silent collective acknowledgment that this was true. "So much so," the Director General continued, though now building on each weighted word, "that it's led to the establishment of a new bureau! The Conceptual Analysis Bureau is to be opened on Day 560 (E2). As Director General of the Law Bureau, I wish the Conceptual Analysis Bureau the very best."

He paused: punctuating his speech and consuming the faces of his small audience. "However," he continued assertively, "it's also my pleasure to announce that the Government expects more than just my good wishes." There were several cameras positioned around the room, and the Director was increasingly dividing his attention with them. Small orange lights on top of the cameras intermittently flashed on and off. The orange light most frequently on was that atop the camera directly facing the Director. Almost ignoring those in the room, his attention now squared on this; in return the camera's light remained steady. "The opening of the Conceptual Analysis Bureau creates many new jobs. The Government plans for many current employees from across *all departments* of the Law Bureau to transfer. Many of the jobs in the new bureau, *including some of the very best*, are reserved for us.

"As pioneers of the law program, as well as relatedly having absorbed the Morality Department of the former Philosophy Bureau, towards the end of cycle D3 shortly before said bureau's dissolution, the Government has commissioned us to commence work on a conceptual analysis computer program. Of course, as with the law program, for those employed for this latest program, you'll be working in close collaboration with the Computer Science Bureau and

Logic Department. So, you'll be pleased to know, this will be an opportunity to work with familiar faces.

"The conceptual analysis computer program will work in much the same way as our law computer program, only the architecture is to contain conceptual content rather than legal. Instead of containing laws and the legal relations thereof, the architecture is to contain certain propositions and the logical relationships therebetween. Instead of processing a legal case, it will process a proposition (or set of propositions). The result of this processing will be an analysis of which other propositions the inputted proposition is logically consistent with – no matter how mutually unrelated said two sets of propositions appear to the human mind. Another objective is to index and reduce problematic conceptual terminology.

"There's no reason why computers can't perform conceptual analysis too, and a lot better than people – or at least," the Director amended his words, "a lot better than people alone: they're the ideal tool for us. Unlike refined computer code, our words have messy semantic histories. Compared with computers, we have a very limited ability to entertain many associations at any one time. Similarly, at any one time, we can entertain lines of deductive reasoning of only very limited lengths.

"This has all contributed to repeated setbacks in the attainment of that elusive dream, of correctly analysing and thereby systematising our human concepts: a subtly powerful key to much more besides." The Director executed the final line with perfect passion: "Computers, ideal for such tasks, are here!" Together with those in the room, and by extension those watching the broadcast through the cameras, Cameron felt part of an enormous circuit charged through with a burst of current. All listened keenly to the Director continue.

"Working in a typical department within the Conceptual Analysis Bureau, you'll work closely with the respective bureau or department for which the concepts thereof your department is responsible for analysing – for example, the Physics Conceptual Analysis Department will work closely with the Physics Bureau – for the primary purpose of improving field theoretical understanding, thereby facilitating field progress. Moreover, of archetypal importance, being part of one and the same bureau, and working on the same *holistic* computer program, naturally you'll also work closely with other departments within the Conceptual Analysis Bureau, generally for the purpose of aiding interdisciplinary progress, via communication and efficient collaboration between *all* bureaus." First stepping back, as if to take in the totality of all which had passed, the Director then took his seat.

The light atop the camera facing Cameron flashed on. Before cameras were introduced, he used to like meetings. Realising the camera was focused in the direction of a woman, farther up the table, he became less self-conscious. She stood up and was about to ask a question. For this type of meeting the cameras would be broadcasting only to the offices in the Law Bureau. Everyone watching knew the woman's question was staged. However, it still had its purpose as it helped refocus attention. "Won't suitable candidates for jobs in the Conceptual Analysis Bureau typically require non-legal specialist knowledge?" The Director General stood up and was quick to reply, "No. Don't be discouraged at lacking such knowledge. Again, it's largely due to our unique knowledge of and experience with our computer program and system that the Government's interested in us, notably in relation to the process of inputting and analysing content. However, be prepared to learn something new."

The Director General sat down once more, ready for more questions. There being none he again stood up and concluded his brief speech. Everyone now realised this had been the sole purpose of the meeting. "In this unprecedented project, in accordance with the results thereof, the very compositions of bureaus and departments potentially are subject to change! (The names thereof after all themselves represent particular concepts.) Nonetheless, please note that the purposes of the Politics Conceptual Analysis Department are categorically deemed most important; correspondingly, the most job openings will be in said department, wherein you'll notably work closely with the Government itself."

The Director was swiftly keen to conclude the meeting, "Anyone wishing to transfer, please apply through the normal channels. Currently the normal channels in relation to a range of jobs in the Conceptual Analysis Bureau are open only to current Law Bureau employees. In three fifthdays, this will no longer be the case, as the normal channels will be open to all. You are encouraged to take advantage of this excellent opportunity. I congratulate you all as pioneers of the law computer program for having created it for yourselves."

There was a sharp tear in Cameron's reel of experience. Snapped off the back of a void, he rediscovered his body on a bed. Slowly in his cell again, he felt exhausted. He was unable to physically move or control his thoughts. However, he didn't want to move, and his thoughts, peaceful, weren't in need of control. He felt a state of warm and wholesome languor, laced with fresh achievement.

He'd remembered more, and what he'd remembered confirmed his feeling of significance.

I'm in the Law Bureau and the head of a department! I'm fairly sure

The memories didn't yet explain his current circumstances. However, progress was at least coming, and at present this seemed the most real thing to hope for. Naturally, each memory was also cherished for itself.

6 STRANGER

Outside, silk rain threaded down through a breeze; inside, Cameron's mind and lungs breathed its fresh clatter on leafy shapes of green. Lying in his soft white bed, morning greeted him once again. The new day hadn't come easily, and so he was still tired.

He'd woken in the night and spotted the dark fuzzy island which now dominated his floor. Turning back onto his front, he faced both the wall and cool air falling through the window. However, the subtle imprint of what he'd glimpsed appeared to have smudged his mind's eye, which couldn't project dreams cleanly as before.

Cameron eased himself up onto his elbows. Seeing steam rising from a cup on the table beyond the end of the bed, he smelt coffee. Breakfast was waiting for him. He planted his feet on the cold floor beneath and was ready to start his day.

Having finished breakfast, he sat on his sheets, with nothing left but the day ahead. Before him, the grenade lay on the floor. He stood up, and without thinking, walked over and picked it up. He walked back past the foot of the bed. He crouched down. Next, he stretched out his arm and set down the object underneath the table by its back-left leg. Finally, he returned to his bed and sat down. Met with his familiarly plain floor, he seemed to himself content.

it's my grenade after all if it's going to be left in my cell so I can do whatever I want with it, I'm free to move it around… and since I'm the one who never wanted it in here in the first place moving it to an out-of-the-way place is the most rational thing to do

He stood up and paced his cell. He was happy to note the grenade's new home each time he glimpsed it, resting underneath the table, instead of cluttering up his white path across the cell. In time, his body had its fill of walking. Halting, he turned and leant back on the wall behind. Across from him was the toilet. Stood there, large and centred in the light, it fleetingly imposed a throne-like presence. Bored, and reminded he hadn't slept well, he marched up and tried it out as his throne. He noticed that from here the bed partly obstructed his view below the table. He sat back, king of his cell. Soon he was lost in daydream.

Cameron slowly became aware of a faint tapping.

… a message from the sovereign of another land…

Still daydreaming, the sounds only had an impact on his imagination. Barely discernible but undoubtedly there, a slight cadence was present. It had been coming from the other side of the wall behind for some time now.

it's real

The external fact took time to register.

it's real!

In a rush of excitement, Cameron came swiftly back to reality. The sounds were coming from a section of wall low down to his right. He almost fell off the toilet to kneel down to listen better.

that's definitely not random

The deliberate sounds were those of a mysterious fellow member of life and he listened: communication was happening.

He was about to tap back a response but hesitated, initial excitement already expiring into nerves. The tapping from the other side continued as before. However, it had started to change in his imagination. Now it sounded like a dog scratching to be let in. It stopped.

Cameron stayed fixed where he was, waiting, and wondering what he should do. The position he was knelt in wasn't comfortable. He turned and let his legs stretch out with his back to the wall, his thoughts on its other side. He was steadily arriving at the resolution that he would tap something back in response, when new yet familiar sounds came diagonally across from where he was sitting, behind the cell door.

that must be Lucy with lunch

Sure enough, Lucy entered with a silver tray of food. As she rotated back to shut the door, Cameron quickly stood up.

On her walk to the table, Lucy halted, tray in hand, spotting the grenade now placed by its back-left leg. Turning her head, she cast her gaze over down at Cameron's feet, where he'd just been sitting. Next her attention shifted to the bed by the wall, located between Cameron and the table. With a mild smile, "More comfortable sat down there, are we?" she asked, "Come on. Have a seat, lunch is ready." Lucy didn't stay to talk this time. Cameron traipsed across the whiteness to start his meal.

Given little else to do, as well as due to the good quality of the food, he took his time over meals. Even so, like all others, he'd soon finished this particular lunch.

With a full stomach, drowsiness led him to bed. He wasn't in a sleeping mood though. He just wanted to lay his body down and not think on anything much at all, apart from perhaps the meal he'd just enjoyed.

chicken casserole

Head on pillow, he stared blankly at the ceiling. Unlike his limbs, his eyelids weren't heavy. He soon closed his eyes anyway. Met with the film-coloured canvas thereby presented, he noticed smudged, alternating, dark and reddish strips. He recognised these for the imprint of the bars in his window just above. Further surveying the dark and murky scene, scattered falling movements attracted his attention. In this way, some of time passed that day.

It was sounds of tapping that hailed him back out and into the world of original light. On a horizontal plane, they were coming from directly above the crown of his head.

it's the same as before

Cameron was in the same slightly awkward kneeling position, as before, with his ear to the wall. Again, there was a definite cadence in the taps. Yet he was developing doubts about their suggestions of sentient communication. A sharp human whisper struck through the wall, seemingly shattering a dividing pane, "Hsss, I'm John."

Taken by surprise, Cameron thought he'd jumped back. In fact, he'd gently toppled over onto his hands and forearms. Stunned, and anxiously aware his track on time had snagged, he hastily spluttered out a reply, "Hello!… John?… Cameron – I'm Cameron." "Hello, Cameron, I'm John."

"You live here too?" asked the voice. "Yes, I suppose so," replied Cameron. "You don't work here though, do you?" "No, I don't work here." "So what's your job then?" "… I—" "Or I mean what's your *role* here?" Cameron's thoughts paused. "… I'm—well, I don't know, I mean I don't think I really have a role as such." The questions were oddly difficult. Just in time before the next one came, Cameron was quick to add, "How about you?" "Our roles are the same I suppose," was the reply. The voice seemed happy to wait for the next question. "How long have you lived here for?" asked Cameron. "Yes, I do live here, like you. I've been here since I can remember."

Cameron sat upright on hearing this, forgetting any initial shyness. "Yes – I'd say I've been here since I can remember too!" he whispered back. He wondered if he'd assumed too much. "Have you lost your memory too then?" asked the voice. "Yes, that's what I meant," Cameron answered, timidly. "It's not so bad here after all though, is it?" the voice went on. "The food's good!" offered Cameron.

They shared more silence together. "John?" "Yes?" Now Cameron didn't know what to say. His mind's undercurrents were strong on the mutual loss of memory he and his neighbour had in common. He wanted to talk more about this, perhaps even share the two memories he'd recovered since he'd woken up here, "So you woke up here too?… One day?… And you realised you didn't really know where or what you were?" Cameron started. "Yes, yes, exactly the same," the voice replied.

"But you know," it went on keenly, "I've woken up in the night and heard voices – I mean – a recording." "A recording?" "Yes. I've only heard it twice. The first time I heard it, I sat up in bed wondering what the noise was. But having sat up, before I had a chance to listen, it cut out. But I knew it was a human voice – right here in my room. How about that then? Though as I fell back to sleep, I started to doubt if it was real and wondered if I was going mad… Cameron?" "Yes?" "Well, I woke up the next day, and in the morning found myself sure that I wasn't mad – not yet," the voice thinly chuckled at the idea, "and as the day went on, I wondered more on what had happened the night before. And I felt sure I'd heard a recording of someone talking to me in my sleep – and it was a woman's voice – and so of course I wanted to know what she was saying."

The voice interrupted itself, "Have *you* heard recordings of a woman talking to you in your sleep?" Cameron was asked.

recordings in my sleep…

"No, I haven't. But I'm curious, like you were, what was on the recording – did you find out?" The prompt made it through the steel.

"That same following night I tried to stay up, or at least sleep lightly, in order to hear the words on the recording. But I had no luck, and all that happened was I didn't sleep well. The next night my body made up for the loss of sleep from the night before, so I had no chance of listening out for the recording then either. But I was still determined. The following day, I drank a little more water than usual before I went to bed, planning that this would wake me up in the night, when the recording might be playing…

"And it worked! Waking up, I was about to turn over and open my eyes, when I heard the woman's voice on the recording and caught myself just in time. I knew I was in my cell – and sensed it was dark, though my eyes were still closed – and I remembered what I was about. I recalled how last time when I'd sat up, the recording had almost immediately cut out. So this time, I didn't dare move. I lay perfectly still – aside from breathing steadily – and pretended to still be asleep. But of course, I wasn't: I listened, as best I could from the position I was in." From his side of the wall, Cameron did the same.

"So, what was the woman saying?" Cameron asked. "Her voice was slow and monotone," came back the reply, "There was no feeling in any of the words. But it was all about being rational. I can remember the words exactly: 'Think rationally. Live rationally. Be rationally.' That was what I first woke to. And it was being repeated over and over. I don't know how long it had been going on for before I woke up. But after a short while or so, it stopped. And a new cycle of repetitions began.

"The same recorded monotone voice went on as before. But this time, I'd say the content was stranger: 'Philosophy is *not* spontaneous. Live by a good system. Programs have no regrets.' The word 'not', in the 'Philosophy is *not* spontaneous' part, was in a deeper tone, as if to emphasise it – or *de-*emphasise it. So I suppose in a sense that part wasn't monotone – but the rest was… No, I mean, if it wasn't for that one word, then it would've all been monotone. Yes, that's how to put it." Cameron repeated back the words on the recording. They rolled off his tongue quite naturally. "That *is* strange," he agreed, hoping his neighbour could explain it.

"After a while," the voice continued, "it seemed like those same words had been repeating on and on forever… especially perhaps, because at that point I was now desperate to use the toilet! But I didn't want to let on that I'd been awake listening. I decided I'd wait to hear another five repetitions; if the words hadn't changed by the sixth, then I'd sit upright, just as if I'd just woken up – like the first time I heard the recording. The words didn't change, and so that's what I did. And not more than one of those phrases had been said and the recording cut off, just like the first time. So I got up (wary not to appear too desperate to go) and went. And that was that. And I've not heard that voice in the night since, not consciously anyway."

Both sides went into private discussion with himself. Cameron didn't want to share his memories with this stranger any more. Something stopped him. It was the same reason he hadn't shared them with Lucy. They might get battered and bruised out in the open. If this ultimately strengthened them, or even hammered them into a new shape, that would be OK; if they were somehow destroyed, he might not bear it. His mind drifted near such thoughts – but at a safe distance, where they were too far off to be read clearly.

"Is there a grenade in your cell?" There was no answer. "John?" "Yes?" "In your cell… is there a grenade?" Cameron asked again. "What? – No – What do you mean? A grenade? How could I be left with a grenade?… Why? Is there one in yours?" asked the voice. Cameron looked towards his bed. Looking over it, his vision focused on the top of the table, its straight white edge level with his eyes. "Yes," he confessed, "but I don't want it in here with me." "But why not?" shot back the response, with a hint of irritation, "You could use it to escape." "What kind of escape would that be? How? To where?" retorted Cameron. "Oh, I don't know, use your imagination. Do they let you carry it with you when there's a cell change?" Answering its own question, "No, surely not, that would be too easy!"

"What do you mean 'a cell change'?" questioned Cameron. "What do you mean, 'what do I mean'? When you're escorted to a new cell – don't tell me they let you walk around the corridors here with a working grenade on your hands!?" exclaimed the voice, "You do mean a *working* grenade, don't you? You're sure?" "I haven't seen the corridors here," explained Cameron, a little insecurely. "But what about when you go for meals?" he was asked, incredulously. "Lucy brings me my meals… and I have them at my table, in the corner at the end of my bed."

"Lucy?" "Yes, you know, the guard." "Lucy, yes, yes, I know. Lucy. Well, she *calls* herself a carer but—" The voice cut off its speech and Cameron cut in, "I didn't call her a carer; I said she was the guard. What though? 'But' what?" Not wanting to sound rude, Cameron elaborated, "I didn't hear what you said?" Wrapped in hushed tones, the words were smuggled through the wall, "She's a dangerous woman." "What do you mean? She's my friend," affirmed Cameron. "Hello?" No answer came back.

Cameron soon realised he was talking to himself. Turning his head back, he saw a turquoise figure standing by the door. It was Lucy. She gestured to the table on which was placed dinner. In her hands was a tray with the used cutlery from lunch. "Good night, see you in the morning," she said warmly, from her place by the door. After a pause reserved for Cameron unused, she quietly exited, the rectangular white door closing after her.

7 OPAQUE MEETING

"On the agenda is the problem of prison overcrowding." Two large and vacant grey eyes flashed. "Our team is still working on the introduction of death, as a sentence, into the legal system. It was expected this would take a while, as death is a new class of sentence. However, we didn't realise it would cause such problems for the program."

Cameron was in another meeting at work. Like last time, apart from the Director General, he didn't pay much attention to the other people in the room. He sensed those around the table were the same and that he was seated at his same place. However, the room was slightly different. The smell of sandalwood softened the air. The space was also a little warmer, and the seats were more comfortable. There were no cameras. There were also no windows, just carefully lit oak panelling. As before, standing at the head of the smooth dark table was the Director General of Law. He seemed less inhuman than in the other meeting.

"This technical issue is taking longer than expected to resolve, and meanwhile the problem of overcrowding is getting worse," he continued. "Again, I'll remind you, we need a short-term solution. Whilst building more prisons, for example, solves the problem, it then leaves us in embarrassment, once the death sentence has been legislated and our need for prison space is lower than ever." Preceded by an inaudible urbane breath, the Director seated himself.

The man in the middle opposite Cameron, still in his seat, started to talk. He was a little overweight and the edge of the top button of his shirt showed, just above the generously large knot of his soft lilac tie. His large face, though presenting acutely intelligent features, had a foolish glaze. "Couldn't we build more prisons, but then convert them once the problem is resolved? They could be converted to schools, for instance, fairly efficiently and at a low cost." "This is an idea," rejoined the Director General tonelessly, "but consider also that they might be converted into museums, which educate the public on how the E3 Director General of Law's famous computer program failed in its promised efficiency targets." Silence corroded the exchange to nothing. The Director waited for more suggestions and everyone else in the room diligently hunted for them.

The thought-bound quiet broke when the Director stood up, curiously only those nearest him apparently not noticing. "This issue is of top priority," he began. "You've all been given plenty of time to think on it, and it's each of your jobs to think on it, but now is no longer the time for thinking in isolation. We're met here together for discussion." As he moved to sit back down, he added, "It's a difficult problem and so all suggestions are welcome," his vacant glance lingering above the large-faced lilac-tie man, who didn't seem to notice.

Cameron heard a body shifting. Following the sound, in the corner of his left eye, he met its source, where he found two grey-suited arms stretched out on the table's slick brown wood. The person sat on his left, leaning forward, was about to speak. "What about the options for reducing crime rates?" a quick male voice asked, "I know it's not a function of the Law Bureau, and among other things, it's one of the main targets for the conceptual analysis program. However," stressing the transition though still in tight pace, "it would help alleviate some pressure, and as of yet the designs for the conceptual analysis computer program haven't even begun.

"Then of course there are minor schemes in action – but these are all somewhat experimental, and the Government clearly doesn't have much confidence in them given the funding that's been made available. Project PR, for example: all the reports suggest religion is too toxic to be a viable solution, even if it's one that's designed, implemented and evolved to 'perfection' by our very best.

"So given we have a guiding role for the new Conceptual Analysis Bureau, in the design of the conceptual analysis computer program – which as I say, one of the main targets of which is the reduction of crime – couldn't we perhaps use this to vindicate engagement in some *preliminary work of our own*, aimed at the reduction of crime, especially as it does indeed marry so well with our problem currently under discussion?"

During the flow of speech, Cameron had sat up straight in his chair, not wanting to get in the way of the Director to his right and the speaker on his left. He'd listened carefully, looking down into the glimmering wood before him, and unaware whether remaining on it to the left were the two grey arms. The room was again in silence. Cameron glanced up to his right.

He wasn't expecting to find that the Director General also wasn't looking at the speaker. He was instead gazing ahead down the length of the large table. "Are there any comments or questions relating to this?" the Director's voice diced the air. Everyone waited for nobody to talk. "Quite," the Director announced, "as you say, it's not our function to reduce crime: that's one of the roles of the Government itself."

Still in his seat, the Director General faced the former speaker with squared shoulders. "Naturally, we follow protocol as always." "Of course, I didn't mean—" chimed in the man, anxiously. "Like *all bureaus*, we are defined by our place within the system we comprise. We do not make an exception of ourselves – whatever the apparent short-term gain, whatever the reason: *all* exceptions are ultimately enemies of systems *on principle*. A rogue bureau is no bureau". "A rogue is no bureau," reiterated the man. "Very good."

Leaning back the Director seemed bored, speaking to no one and everyone, as he provided an exegesis on the former speaker's proposal, "Specifically alluded to is a chief purpose of the

Politics Conceptual Analysis Department of the Conceptual Analysis Bureau: to analyse and counter any composite unfolding of ideas, arguments, representations of events, etc. which are considered potentially threatening to Government policy, ideally supplying the power to consistently counter pre-emptively any trends in various domains of public thought or behaviour which threaten stability, inclusive of public security, and indeed thereby achieving such targets as reducing crime rates."

He stood up, "As was also just highlighted, one of the courses of action involved therein which the Government is taking to reduce crime is to work on a conceptual analysis computer program. This added to the legal results we've already obtained through our law computer program, and then further combined with the legislation of a death sentence, mean prison overcrowding will quite simply be a circumstance of the past – ideally along with, at least as we know them, prisons themselves: the unreformable will be executed and the rest will be law-abiding.

"However, in the meantime," he continued, surveying the room, "although crime rates are already relatively low, overcrowding is a current problem because targets have not been met. Targets have not been met because we have not met our deadline to legislate death as a sentence. Hence, our bureau has been held responsible with this ratio-related problem of overcrowding. It is our job to amend the situation using our legal expertise (not our inexistent expertise in other fields, political or otherwise)." The Director General sat down and waited once again.

Before a new layer of quiet had settled, from the head end of the table, a bold female voice caught the room's attention still out, "What's the latest on when the death problem will be resolved? Relatedly, what of the issue of serial killer cases?" It sounded like the same woman who'd asked the question in the other meeting. However, Cameron wasn't sure; this voice had more life or passion. The woman, having been standing, had already sat down. Cameron made to look down the table, past the line of faces, to see if it was the same woman.

However, as he turned, he was caught by the magnificent stare of the Director General, unsettlingly squared on him. The Director stood up and proceeded to answer the question, still focused on an uncomposed Cameron, as if the question had come from him, "The computer legal system is designed to process cases in terms of finite numbers. This was identified a while ago as a potential problem for incorporating the notion of death into the system; as a sentence, a finite number it seems cannot be used to represent death. By a process of elimination, we are increasingly sure that this is the problem." Cameron uncomfortably gave his full and polite attention, whilst the Director was giving him the answer to a question he hadn't asked. He was relieved when the answer finished.

Yet calm didn't follow. There was a contained bustle from where the original questioner's voice had come. Cameron leant forwards, his eyes quickly jumping up the row. It *was* the same woman. She was about to stand up again. The Director had promptly anticipated her and was already now standing again himself.

As the Director spoke, Cameron looked up and was embarrassed to realise he was looking dead at him, once more. "I'm also happy to tell you about news regarding resolutions to the problem," he began, "– in addition to those already suggested today," he added smiling. "Of course, identifying the problem is the first step. As I've explained, we're now more confident about what exactly that is." He presented the room with a marked pause.

The Director General's eyes, two perfect spheres, remained fixed on Cameron. "We've experimented with altering the different numerical values, which represent different sentences, to see if there's a combination whereby the death sentence can be incorporated into a reformed system. The beauty of the system is that the mass of information is all logically connected, in ways a human mind is incapable of conceiving. However, this is simultaneously a problem when it comes to introducing something 'radically new' into it: everything may be affected.

"Specifically, the results of all the different experiments fall into two types: either we keep coherence, but the system as a whole becomes too counterintuitive and inexpedient to be justifiable; or we lose consistency. In either case, ultimately the system does not deliver justice."

The Director released his pin on Cameron and breezed his attention around the room, "I've met with the Director General of the Mathematics Bureau, and a specialist in set theory is being sent here to consult with our team. It may be that the only solution is to redesign the entire computer legal system. This is a perfectly good option. It can be done in tandem with the new design of the conceptual analysis computer program. The only issue is this will be a relatively long time coming, *which is why*," he added, leaning forwards, "we have the problem which is on the agenda for today." He looked down at the woman on his left as he sat down.

The Director General was in his seat again. There was a recurrence of the same contained bustle as before. The Director's head rotated to his left to let his eyes watch what was there. The bustling stopped.

"John?" said the Director, as if the name was a proposal. He turned, surveying the table, going up along Cameron's row, past the opposite end of the table, and then back down the line of faces on the other side. His eyes presently met the man directly to his right.

"John": the name was familiar, as was the man's bearded face. Cameron waited to see if the voice was too.

"Do you have any suggestions, John?" asked the Director. He spoke to this man differently. The Director's expression exhibited some hope of a tangible benefit from the interaction. The Director and Cameron both waited for the man to speak. The man shrugged apologetically. Cameron looked back to see the Director's response. Whilst the thoughts of the room still loitered around the moment just gone, the Director's had already surged on.

He stood up ominously. "Before I continue, I'd like to remind you all: this is an opaque meeting," he stated firmly, inspecting the expressions of the room. The atmosphere changed. Everyone waited, as if for something heavy falling to smack the ground.

"Another suggestion for discussion: incited suicide." He continued steadily on, preventing the room from gauging its reaction to the marriage of the two words, "Reports show that a relatively high proportion of criminals are highly *impulsive*." The Director paused generously on the final word, allowing any initial comments.

"There is an opportunity here to operate, in our capacity as the Law Bureau, outside the current computer legal system and yet without violating the law. As I hope we all see it now, these are criteria for a solution to our problem. It's a temporary solution to the problem of prison overcrowding, whilst we wait for the legislation of the death sentence.

"The much-needed solution, which is currently under discussion for us all, is to incite the suicides only of those criminals who under the future legal system will most certainly be sentenced to death, once the technical glitches are resolved. As with current standard legal practice, the computer program processes all cases. However, using the old system, we can additionally manually assess individually what would be likely death-sentence cases within the new system. As appropriate, we then attach the order for the prison authorities. The prison authorities then carry out the order, within the confines of the law."

The Director looked ahead, and assuming an almost admonishing tone, "So, for instance, the prisoners cannot be lied to, or given the means to commit the act of suicide under the influence of intoxicants and so on… well, I won't lecture those of us here on the law," he added, looking around, "but such issues should be contemplated. The Morality

Department may be dissolved but we still have morals," he closed, with an admirably easy smile.

On the soft cell pillow, Cameron's brain was finding it difficult to digest in real time all that was said. Force-fed on the Director's words, whatever line of reasoning there was, it hadn't got through complete, and with large wet chunks of experience arriving in his stomach, now he felt sick.

A man sitting somewhere asked the Director a question, "How exactly would it work?" The Director was quick to engage him. "As for the 'inciting' element of the concept, I've been in consultation with the Director General of Animal Science. We've devised a reasonably efficient means, using psychology which is legally compliant. As for the 'suicide' element, we are considering different options." The Director was looking at Cameron, again, as if he'd asked the question. He felt pale. "Of course, the two elements (of inciting the suicide using cutting-edge psychology, and deciding how to provide the best physical means for the act to be performed) also need to be considered in combination.

"However, first, to take the 'suicide' element by itself. It mustn't endanger others." Cameron felt the Director enjoying his paleness, as with a draining effort he met his eyes. His face was very close. It felt like a different time and place, in which they were alone. The Director's voice sliced his ear drums before seeping in, "Secondly, it must be something that doesn't maim but kills instantly every time."

Up close the Director's eyes were vivid grey. Yet, at the same time, how could they still be so vacant? Cameron realised he'd seen eyes like it before: they were the eyes of a dead animal.

Something urgent rescued Cameron from the scene. Pulled up through suffocation into open air, he was sitting up rigidly in bed. It was night air. It was cold and fresh. Finding it hard to breathe and too eager to, he'd gulped in too much oxygen and his lungs hurt, the inhaling sound he'd just made got trapped in his head. He thrust himself out of bed and stumbled to the wall opposite, making to walk off the abrupt inhalation. His eyes stung, as though sharp crystals were mingled with his sweat. Now turning back from the wall and wiping his eyelids, he proceeded to continue his stumbled pacing, when with a voiceless shout his whole body jerked back, like a trekker about to tread on a viciously poised snake. The grenade had appeared in his path, faintly black-red in the darkness. In his doubled shock and confusion, he lost consciousness, collapsing by a cold white wall and into blackness.

Waves of dawn light arrived to draw Cameron out from his blank sleep on the steel floor. Shivering, he was thirsty. The water fountain was distant. In the half-light haze, his legs were already carrying him directly to bed. He ignored the grenade, lacking the energy to host emotion, and crawled into white sheets. Slowly there was gentle warmth. As he passed out, his mind was dimly concerned with a need to do something.

8   PSYCHIATRIST

Cameron found his coffee already cold when he sat down to eat breakfast. After last night, it seemed days since reality was again real. He sipped a little at the milky brown liquid and finished his fruit salad.

Sitting on his bed and vaguely refreshed, in front of him on the whiteness lay the grenade. He'd landed back in the all-too-familiar situation, like a recurring nightmare. The vividly dead object expanded before him. The shiny red of the ring pull drew him in only to warn him off. Off guard, he was soon pulled back in again. This back and forth repeated itself with increasing speed, until the yanking in and shunning away became simultaneous. His attention felt caught in a moment so agonisingly stretched that it was ready to rip open.

Cameron tore his head away and swung it onto the pillow, behind where his left hand had just been. His body followed. Hoisting his legs up, he stretched out on the bed. Now his only view was the clear ceiling.

Finally, his mind had some space and time to reflect on the memory of last night.

was it a memory, it was more like a dream… but then my other memories had been like dreams, they'd all been rediscovered by the re-experience of them… but this one had happened at night… but had I been asleep, did that matter

He couldn't give reasoned answers to the questions, but a hefty instinct dragged him to group the experience with his other memories.

incited suicide

Cameron strained to focus on the words of sound-filled ink in his mind. He looked to his left where the grenade hadn't moved. As cloudy ideas converged, his sky became a clear black. A chain of propositions passed quietly through his consciousness.

they want me to kill myself, that's the plan… that's what I'm supposed to do, it's been decided by the Government… that's my sentence… and so after all I'm just a criminal

of course I'm a criminal though! I've been locked up in a prison cell, what else could I be! and of course they want me to kill himself! why else would I be locked up in a small room with nothing to pass the time but a grenade!

It had always been so obvious. He pounced on his dullness, gnashing at it.

Coming back out to his senses, Cameron looked around him with fresh raw eyes. He was trapped inside what he now saw clearly as just the bare steel carcass of an arbitrary prison cell.

but no, it's not just a cell, it's an execution room and I'm the executioner, condemned…

He shot up and rushed over to the grenade angrily. Bent over about to touch it, he jolted, his anger scurrying away in fear. However, the abrupt calm that comes from urgent caution took him, and he picked the object up. It was heavy in his lazy arm and cold in his hot palm. He turned to walk over to the white chair and table. Encountering an impulse to yank out the ring pull, he tightened his free hand into a fist, and twisting his elbow, jerked his arm back.

The impulse still nagged. In his imagination, he'd now already done it: he'd stopped, rooted where he was stood, and waited for the explosion in disgusted terror; next his body was in pieces, weltering silently on a white canvas, mixed with jags of metal; somewhere on the floor was his dead face, contorted with wasted life. The scene was to be discovered by Lucy when she came in as usual with his lunch. The news would soon travel. Other lives would be affected. His final eternal act would have been to forge the confused suffering of those dear to him. As Cameron walked across the white floor, all this awesome possibility existed in a string of instants vibrating with its own tension.

He had made it to the table and was knelt with his hand outstretched. As he released the grenade, his heart thumped his chest. He could relax his concentration now. He straightened back and upwards out from where he was crouching. Carelessly, he knocked his head on the underside of the hard thick steel above. He heard the pain before he felt it. Sat down on his bed again, he rubbed his head.

Although satisfied to see a clear floor, this was no longer enough.

there's a scheme for my destruction

This was the dominant explanation for his circumstances; although some friendly doubts had already been invited in by now, they lacked influence. He had no counteractive schemes of his own.

Plunged in thought, the sounds from behind the door almost didn't reach him. He looked up just in time to see it opening. In a panic, he took counsel with himself. Time slowed generously for him.

there's no need to be rash and let on to her what I know

He reassured himself that his thoughts weren't on display. Calming a little, he greeted Lucy, who turned back from the door with his lunch.

"Good morning," offered Cameron. "Good afternoon," corrected Lucy, her gentle eyebrows rising. "Have you just woken up?" she asked as she walked over to the table. "I took a while getting to sleep last night," explained Cameron. Lucy stopped at the table. Tray still in hand, she looked back at the absent grenade in the centre of the cell. Next, she took a step back to peer beneath the table. She carried on as usual, exchanging the table's cutlery with that of her tray. "Your lunch," she left the words at the steel table with the meal.

Once back at the door, Lucy didn't take out her keys but hesitated. She turned to look under the table again. Cameron imagined she was going to stride over, pick up the grenade and place it back in the centre of the cell. She caught Cameron observing her. Smiling back, "Enjoy your lunch. Sorry I can't stay and chat but I'm quite busy today." She took out her keys and left. Cameron perceived traces of irritation scattering as the door shut. As he ate lunch, a mistrust for Lucy brooded.

Late afternoon found Cameron pacing his cell. He'd come to the conclusion that his problem was a lack of information. He still didn't know enough about who he was, where he was, or why he was here. Even what he did know, he could doubt. Having turned back from the toilet-hosting wall as he paced, his neighbour, John, and their conversation entered his mind. At that moment, he decided that he trusted John.

he can help me

Cameron rushed over to the section of wall to the left of the toilet and sat down. Shifting to his right to face the window, with his arm lowered, he rapped the wall with his knuckle, adding the same mild cadence he'd heard John use. He waited expectantly. There was no answer. He rapped again on the same area of white steel, and whispered through the wall, "John?" Again, he waited but again there was no reply. Sounds came from over by the door. Cameron jumped up, but he quickly realised he'd imagined it.

He resumed his pacing, and thinking, and remembering. Every so often, when his thoughts met dead ends, he'd sit by the wall and try knocking for John but this led nowhere too.

Cameron's world revolved quickly that day, as already the light was dimming and it felt late. Chilling grenade fantasies had made minor ambushes during his efforts to remember. He'd tried to remember more – something new – but had had no luck. Presently, he lay on his bed, bathing in translucent sheets of the last afternoon sunlight. He allowed his mind and body rest, though at the same time was still hopeful he might discover a memory hiding in a doze. However, he encountered nothing.

He came to the resolution to confront Lucy at dinner.

she owes me more of an explanation than she's given

As he gazed up, he was comforted by the prospect of answers before the end of the day. With a new understanding, the situation itself would be transformed.

He started to wish he'd reached the resolution a little later, because time now dragged. Its flow was as reluctant to meet the moment of action as Cameron was keen. Despite Lucy's arrival with dinner being a while yet, already his insides fluttered.

I need to choose my words carefully and keep under control… and I need to control Lucy too, she's slippery lathered in her talk… as soon as she comes in with dinner I'll stand by the cell door and not budge and I won't agree to talk instead after dinner, it'll be better to show the need for talk is more important, it would cost me my advantage of being the only one prepared too

It was dark outside now, and the small bright light in the cell had flicked on: the signal dinner could now arrive at any time. Cameron's stomach and the electric light both nagged at him that Lucy should have been here by now, as if he decided it.

At last, the sounds of keys hovered somewhere in the corner. Cameron stood up from where he was perched on the bed. He walked across to the opposite wall to face the white rectangle of door. Arriving at his new position, on cue, Lucy entered.

Cameron experienced her entrance routine in slow motion. Turning back to him, with time returning to normal speeds, she smiled, "Dinner!" She garnished the announcement with commentary as she took the tray to the table, "You'll like this one. Roast pheasant. A real treat for you!" Her voice was full of vicarious pleasure.

She set the tray of food on the table. Finding Cameron stood by the door, Lucy finally paid attention to the expression on his face. "Cameron?" "Lucy, we need to talk," said his hollow voice. "Are you OK? What's troubling you?" He stood motionless, re-gathering his words. "What would you like to talk about?" Lucy added, interrupting his thoughts. "This!" he exclaimed, splaying his arms out to the cell.

A seal broken, his speech surged out, "I woke up here one day, without any idea of who or where I am. I don't have any idea of the past. I don't know why I'm here. And already it's been days now and nothing's changed. What about those questions? – 'What is it? Description. Purpose. How's it used?' You said they were part of a procedure to get me out of here? *What* procedure? Things just go on and on:

eating and sleeping, and waking and eating! Yes, and get me out of here *how*? Well yes, some things *have* changed I suppose."

this isn't how I rehearsed it

"That!" he went on, pointing to the grenade by Lucy's heels. Her feet shifted to turn. "What's the meaning of it?!" he shouted, anger crumbling his barriers. "Do you want me to kill myself? Is that it? Blow my body to pieces in a horrible explosion!? Well? What is this place? Is it a prison? Is it some kind of sick experiment? Am I a criminal? Have I done something wrong to deserve this? Have I gone mad?" The questions loitered in the past air like a bunch of rejects. "Answer me!" he yelled.

At the end of the rant, Cameron found himself in her face, panting, his hands clutching at clothing.

my own shirt, not hers

"Say something," he added, less loudly, taking a step back. He retreated to the door. "There," he said over his shoulder bitterly, "that's what I wanted to talk to you about." Back at his post, he faced her again.

Lucy returned quietness. Her gaze fell. She was considering what had been said, weighing the meaning of its emotion. Her bearing now told she'd reached a juncture, but the quietness continued. She was assessing if Cameron had had enough time to calm down before they both went on.

She took a step forward, "OK —" She discontinued the idea and made a half-turn back, bringing both their attention to the hot meal on the table, "Look, I understand you need to talk… but why don't we talk after dinner?" She was walking towards him now, "You obviously have a lot you want to talk about, and we can talk properly then."

The words, distracting him as she approached the guarded door behind, gave her reassuring expression a chance to almost move him out the way. Cameron caught himself: freezing his actions until he'd consulted all his thoughts. He felt a gentle hand flatly press his arm into his ribcage. He looked up and into Lucy's entreating face. "No!" he said at it. He moved his trapped arm in a semicircle back and out, "No, no, no. I'm not hungry. Dinner isn't important – didn't you hear any of what I said? I want to talk *now*. I want you to answer my questions *now*… please."

Lucy stepped backwards away from Cameron. She turned and walked towards the bed, sat down and waited. Even her eyes were still, set on the clear floor before them. "What do you want to know?" she said, not looking up. "Everything I've just asked," shot back Cameron. Lucy was unresponsive.

"Why is *that* in here with me? Why am I locked up in a prison cell, alone, and with a grenade?" he asked. "I'm sorry, I don't understand the problem you have with the grenade?" she replied. Both of them waited. "It's perfectly safe. No one's going to come in and blow you up," Lucy restarted, reassuringly. "What if I pulled it though – accidentally or in my sleep?" Lucy looked confused. "Anyway," continued Cameron hotly, "you still haven't answered my question. What's it doing in here in the first place? It's ridiculous! I don't want it. Take it away with you now, please." He saw the short answer formulating on Lucy's face. "Why not?!" he shouted.

Lucy went quiet again. However, it was a different quiet to before. She stood up tensely to face him, "Your dinner will go cold." A rush of language filled Cameron's mind, but he clenched his tongue.

I'll stay quiet and not talk, then she'll *have to talk, I'm not stupid*

Understanding his reticence, Lucy's voice turned colder, "I've already told you it's not for me to move it about." "Well, who moved it in here then?" "It's not mine," proceeded Lucy, ignoring him. "Well, it's not mine either," countered Cameron. He refocused their attention, "So what's it doing in my cell?"

Lucy went mute. It drew him in and was disquieting.

"*Your* cell?" she said at him, piercing the now-glassy silence. Lucy's nostrils flickered. From beneath, red lightly smeared the white skin of her flat cheeks. "This cell has been provided for you!" she boomed. Cameron flinched back into air which only just before was thinly settled around his shoulders. "The ingratitude. The clean bed sheets and clothes, the provisions for hygiene, the security, the electricity… the work," she added, gesturing to herself. Her unravelling words weighed heavy with disgust. "The food!" She appealed to the meal on the table. "And yes, the pheasant and all the rest has gone cold now." She walked over to demonstrate with a closer look. "The water…

"And also yes, it just so happens a grenade's been provided too. So what? And you don't like it?

And you don't know why it's here? Well, tough… Why do you need to know? And you keep moving it around as if it's yours, even though you complain that you don't want it!" Lucy picked up the grenade and marched it back over to the centre of the cell.

She glanced up into his face. Cameron thought he saw a sneer of triumph glimmer, and a fresh burst of anger flashed inside him. "I don't want any of that!" he shouted, thoughtlessly, "I didn't ask for any of it! I just want some answers and you still haven't given me any!" Lucy closed some of the space between them intimidatingly. Trepidation tugged his anger to back down.

"I'm still not clear about what exactly you want from me." She measured her words like a general negotiating with the enemy. "I don't know who you seem to think I am or what I'm able to tell you?" "Then get me someone else," retorted Cameron, callously, "someone who *can* give me straight answers." He gained satisfaction from the new roles his lines implied. "I want to speak to whoever's in charge of all this," he announced.

Lucy strode over to the door. Cameron had since moved from his sentry post there. He found he was opposite the bed as he watched her leave. Lucy didn't look at him as she left and he didn't try to stop her go.

Cameron was lying in bed, looking at the ceiling. Although it was late, the light was still on. In his periphery, Lucy's face appeared over in the corner. She stood rigidly in front of the door, soft in the light behind her. Cameron hadn't noticed her enter the cell.

She broke the fatigued quiet which had descended on the artificially lit room, "The psychiatrist will come to see you tomorrow. He's not always in because he's a busy man with other work to do. You're fortunate." Her eyes consented to make contact with Cameron's. "He's in charge here. You can ask him your questions." Finished with her errand, she left. The door quietly shut behind her.

Cameron got up, roused awake at a late hour and not knowing what to do.

the light's still on

He was standing out on the floor when the light snapped out. Instantly, it was the dead of night. He doubled back towards the bed, and then turned back around. Completing a rearward step, he let his body fall from the hips, back through black air. His hands were splayed out behind him, ready to catch the bed as a seat. Still in flight, time slowed, as his mind began to fill with ideas about the man he was to meet tomorrow.

* * *

At a chic white tablecloth covering a small table, Cameron was seated in the day. Neatly laid on the flat cotton surface were small white plates, gleaming wine glasses, green serviettes and silverware. The thronging noise of conversations filled the open space. Beams of light were at home as they bounded freely through an enormous glass wall, some staying to play on bright walls which stretched up in defiance of a ceiling. Through the glass, the bustling restaurant expanded out into a large balcony area. Brought in by busy waiters as they briskly passed by, the freshness of the outside air told of how high everyone was amid the blue sky.

Cameron's table was set for two and another man sat opposite. He had a clean-shaven plain face and thin fair hair combed to the side. They were seated to have lunch together on the top floor of a Government building at a place popular with the elite. Behind the man's glasses were kind, sharp eyes. This was Cameron's friend. He was the Assistant Director General of Animal Science. He was a psychiatrist. His name was John, and he was talking.

They hadn't been seated long, and faster than usual, the conversation had fallen on John's favourite topic: work. Cameron never minded this. He found John's work especially interesting, unfortunately more than his own.

"There've been some new developments with the rational implants," proceeded John's considered voice. This was one of his preferred headlines for the topic. This time it sounded like he had some important news. Not in need of prompting, he went on, "Well, you'll recall it's been almost two fifthdays now since the very first implants were installed in the Group A volunteers." "Yes, of course," Cameron replied. He was about to repeat something congratulatory but thought better of it. His friend seemed a little agitated just now.

A waiter arrived with the wine. Glancing up onto his trim uniform, Cameron's ears retuned to the surroundings. The two friends paused their conversation, whilst the waiter poured the cold beige liquid into their large glasses. Having placed the bottle in a cooler on the white tablecloth, the waiter left.

"Last Fourthday," resumed John, "two out of the five didn't show up for the appointed checkup and interview." He lacked his usual enthusiasm when discussing work, and Cameron wondered why he'd started the topic. His friend's face told him he was tired, whilst his voice told him he'd already talked about this endlessly with colleagues in meetings. Cameron interjected to lighten the tone early, "So constantly showing up to checkups and interviews as a lab rat isn't the most rational way to live a human life, is it?" He quickly saw his mistake. "I thought that's what you wanted from them" he added, appeasingly. Cameron had already settled into a more sincere tone, hastily adopted, "– to live rationally, whatever the unexpected results?"

"It's illegal, Cameron," replied John, looking at Cameron as if he himself were a criminal. "They're breaking their contracts with the Government by not attending. It goes against the fundamental principles our entire society's based on… How can it ever be rational to break the law?" Unintended by John, the question hovered angrily. Looking distracted, he picked up his wine glass. He looked into it as he took a healthy swig. Slowly, he once again looked across at Cameron. He was shamefaced to see he'd struck embarrassment into his younger friend, "I'm sorry, I didn't mean to talk to you like that. There's been a lot of stress recently," he explained.

Perhaps he'd spoken like that because it was the next best manner to a nervous one. It was a dangerous question and John knew it, especially now it was being repeated, "So how can it ever be rational to break the law?" he asked quietly. He'd asked a second time. The defence that it was rhetorical was now invalid. At least not to leave it naked, John was quick to dress it with justifications, "We've checked everything: the biochemistry; the software's already tried and tested; there appear to be no problems with the hardware; and as for the operations themselves, they went smoother than expected... We're back to the start," he concluded dejectedly.

The waiter arrived with lunch. He placed the large white plates before each of them, "The swordfish." Cameron was reminded how John always had whatever he was having. They began their lunch with some casual conversation about food. The two friends soon felt more at ease again.

"I still don't know why we're not sat outside on a day like this," said John, looking out beyond the glass wall. "It's too hot," explained Cameron. John was usually happy to go along with the preferences of others, but he'd protested about this before. He looked at Cameron, thinking, and didn't seem to hear his answer. "It's cooler in here," added Cameron, who took a sip of wine.

Cameron took up the main topic again, "I'm sorry to hear that about the implants. But it's a setback, surely – not back to the start? What about the two that did show up? Two out of five is better than nothing." For a moment, he wished he'd said less again. Although if he'd seen irritation dart across his friend's face, it had vanished too quickly and without any traces to be sure. "Maybe, yes... But there's more," John replied. He was leaning forwards and lowering his voice. Anywhere outside the boundary of their table, his words would be swept away in the surrounding hubbub, "Of the two that did show up… all traces of their having ever had implants… have disappeared." Having imparted the information, John leant back to absorb his friend's reaction.

A black screen without depth was before Cameron. He quickly discovered that everywhere he looked, it enveloped his vision. He was sitting just as he had been, but everything had disappeared. "John?"

where's John and the restaurant, power cut? no, sunlight had been streaming in through the glass wall

He turned to his right to look at where the wall had been. To his left, his fingers met with something soft having pliant volume.

a cushion? pillow?

He looked behind him. A blurry barred-window appeared. The surrounding darkness gradually took shape.

I'm back, I must have been sat on the bed all this time

Cameron lay back, pulled the sheets over him, and slept.

* * *

It was a sunny afternoon in the cell. Cameron had already eaten his lunch, and Lucy had already come and gone to take the used cutlery away. They'd talked, but only enough to be civil. She had told him to expect a visit from the psychiatrist that same afternoon. Cameron was sitting on his bed waiting for him, going through the events of the previous day. He'd already moved the grenade back to its place under the table after breakfast. So now before him, the floor was clear.

There was a knock at the door. Cameron felt unprepared. For some reason he'd expected him to be late.

why is he knocking, strange, no one else has ever knocked before, is it him

The same knock was repeated but louder. Cameron jumped up, "Yes?" His word floated pathetically and he would've willingly disowned it. He started to walk towards the door, "Hello?… Come in, please." Keys entered a lock. He'd said enough, and quickly returned to sit back down on the bed. As he looked up, a man was entering the cell. It was the same man as before at the restaurant.

John! an old friend!

He looked a little different. He wasn't clean-shaven this time but had some stubble. John turned around to face the cell. He looked either older or much more tired. He didn't look at Cameron. He walked over to the table and took up the chair. He set the chair down in the centre of the cell to face Cameron.

Making himself comfortable, John addressed him, "Hello, John. How are you today?" It was an increasingly surreal situation.

did I hear right, he called me John, but he's John, did he say hello to me or introduce himself just now

"John?" queried Cameron. "Yes," John replied warmly, "that's your name." "Sorry. What do you mean? – You mean *your* name? – I'm Cameron," said Cameron. Confusion pinched John's eyebrows as he sat back in the chair, "Would you tell me your name again, please?" "Cameron," Cameron replied, wondering at his friend. The residual uncertainty on the psychiatrist's face gradually cleared. His tired eyes patiently discerned the marks of Cameron's expression.

He leant forwards from his chair with an outstretched hand, looking Cameron in the eye delicately, "My name is Dr Cameron." He took Cameron's hand in his own and added his other carefully over both, "Your name is John." He let the sounds register as speech, before releasing the introductory handshake.

Cameron sat in out-of-focus surroundings. His core had been touched. He felt compelled to argue back and fight for his name, but he was defenceless. A fact then charged in to rescue him, "But I've always been called Cameron," Cameron explained, "You can ask Lucy, she knows. She's always called me Cameron and no one's ever called me anything else: it's my name." "Ms Marshvale calls you

Cameron?" The psychiatrist asked himself, sounding alarmed. "Lucy. Yes, I told you," replied Cameron, gaining some genuine confidence now. "Did Lucy tell you your name was Cameron?" Cameron was asked with concern.

Cameron opened his mouth but the man on the bed didn't say anything. "Well, no," as the words stumbled out, his cheeks heated, "I introduced myself." "Naturally, as we all do," responded the psychiatrist, "Well, it's an unfortunate misunderstanding then: one that of course any of us is sorry to have happened." The comment had the desired effect, alleviating the man's embarrassment, "Lucy didn't want to contradict you. But I'm afraid I now must, and assure you that your name is John," he said, conclusively. "I'm Dr Cameron," he added.

Taking palm from chest, the psychiatrist stretched his wrist out from the white sleeve of his coat to look at his watch, "I'm sorry, John, but I'm very busy at the moment. Ms Marshvale said there was something you wanted to talk with me about?"

The man didn't know what to say. Being rushed only further scattered the building blocks for complete thoughts. The psychiatrist walked over to the table and crouched down. He walked back to the white steel chair having retrieved something. He sat down and held out his open hand. From his seat on the bed, all the man's attention focused on the black and red object placed in the air on the fleshy platform.

the grenade

Speech came back to him.

"Yes, exactly," he began, "What's the meaning of it? Why is there a grenade in my cell? Why am I in a cell with a grenade?" His words came out mild but complaining. With more emotion he asked, "Why have I lost my memories?" "You've asked me a lot of questions, perfectly reasonable ones I agree. It seems you're especially concerned about the grenade. You don't like it, do you? Would it be fair to say that you're afraid of it?" He examined the man's reaction and offered back what he saw there, "Well, not afraid, but uncomfortable?" "Yes," agreed the man, "uncomfortable," feeling more secure, "I'm not happy with it." "Whatever we call it," explained the psychiatrist, in a clear voice, weighing the object smoothly from his wrist, "it's in your interests to overcome it." He watched the man, "In a sense, you're simply here with what has always been yours: yours to overcome."

The psychiatrist slowly and quietly stood up. He moved the chair back to its place at the table. He walked back to the centre of the cell. At eye level, the man spotted the grenade was still in his hand. "So, I'd like you to leave this here, please. You'll find things are easier than if you keep moving it back under the table. Trust me." Moving steadily, he placed the black object carefully on the white floor.

"But what if it kills me!?" the man burst out. The psychiatrist squinted at the sunlight between the bars of the window above the man's head, waiting for the question to evaporate. The man stood up. "John? John… I mean Cameron – Dr Cameron – What if it kills me?

"I thought we were friends. I know we are. I've remembered it." Dr Cameron turned away to the right, transplanting his expression onto the cold wall there. As he turned back, looking up, his weary face was dappled with melancholy. "Please, don't make so much effort to remember the past," he urged the man, "Our relationship is strictly professional." A yearning silence stretched between the two men.

"If you need to talk again, then you can tell Lucy and I'll make the time." He solemnly walked to the door to make his exit. The door was open. An urgent faceless creature came blistering through the man's stream of consciousness: "What if it kills me!?" he repeated loudly, "What if I don't overcome it?" He marched towards the door but it was too late. Dr Cameron had already pivoted around, the bottom of his white coat barely tracing the event in a shallow arc. Oblivious of the man, the door was pulled shut from the other side. "What if it blows up!?" the man hurled after his visitor through the white rectangle. He banged on the steel but knew it was no use.

9 ESCAPE

John was lying on his bed looking up, as if through the dimming sunlight, he saw his thoughts on the white ceiling. They centred on the events of the past couple of days, through which he'd acquired his new name.

After the psychiatrist's exit, left stranded at the door, the man was exhausted. His constituents all nagged him incessantly to lie down. He climbed into bed, and quickly comfortable, emotional exhaustion found its edge; he fell through vivid half-dreams into a heavy sleep.

It was morning when he woke and still early. Even so, breakfast was already waiting for him at the table, steam rising proudly through the dawn. He hadn't eaten since lunch the day before. His stomach was empty.

The food and coffee were in every possible way satisfying. However, animal needs met, other concerns slowly re-congregated. Landing himself on the bed, he was pleased to still be sleepy. Before his thoughts had a chance to start with anything, he was dreaming again.

Later the same day, familiar sounds at the door heralded Lucy's arrival with lunch. The man was sitting on the bed awake. He'd already moved the grenade from the centre of his floor. However, this time, he'd moved it to the corner diagonally across from the table, to the right of the steel toilet. It was both out of the way and yet still in the open.

a compromise

He was anxious about Lucy's reaction. It was just one among a network of anxieties about encountering Lucy again. Regret had caught hold of him. For whatever reason, things had gone bad between them. He wanted to start afresh. His premonitions knew the relationship was tainted, but together he and Lucy might keep this secret. First however, the man needed to confront her about his name.

Entering the cell, Lucy's eyes were cast down on the tray of food in her hands for delivery. Her shoulder stayed close to the wall, as she beelined across the white floor surface to the table. Watching her, the man felt faint aggression at this unusual aura. He let her complete her task, before speaking.

"Lucy?" "Yes?" she answered, for the first time looking at him. "My name's John, isn't it?" Lucy waited, before replying, "Yes, your name is John." "Then why have you been calling me Cameron all this time?" he asked, still calmly. "Because that's what you called yourself." The lack of any apology provoked him, "I've lost my memory, Lucy – had you not noticed?!" He quickly regained control. "And so, your name *is* Lucy, is it?" "Yes, of course," she answered. "Oh it still is, how nice for you," the man rejoined, bitterly. He felt better now.

"Your lunch is ready. It's beef casserole. I hope you like it," Lucy explained. "Yes, thank you." Lucy walked to the door. "It's a shame about things before," he called after her. He restrained himself from adding more. "Enjoy your lunch, John," said Lucy, turning back from the unlocked door. She left.

The light from outside continued to fade the hue of the ceiling, which now took John's attention more fully as he gazed up from his bed below. The light inside the cell would be switched on soon.

He sat up and out of his current reflections. They'd left the head on his shoulders more stoic.

there's only so much I can do, maybe now it's all been done

He was resigned to wait for whatever might happen. Yet he was hopeful: not about anything in particular, not even the future; it was purely abstract.

Noises to his left gently tapped at and cracked open his reverie.

tapping!

It was coming from behind the white steel to the left of the toilet.

the same as before, my neighbour, John!

Already he was slumped against the hard wall, his head arched over towards the floor so as to hear better.

"Hello?" said John. "Hello!" came the familiar voice from the other side, excitedly, "It's me! Is that me?" "Hello. Sorry?… Yes, it's you – so how are you?" "Oh never mind that – You know anyway! So you're me then, yes?" It was a genuine question, not just a strange greeting. John struggled with a response, "It's me… John – well, I used to—" "Yes! Excellent!" screeched the voice, "It's worked! I sound like that then? Listen, as you know – or we know – I'm on the other side of this wall, in the regular cell." The voice's speech had bounded along quickly, but already it started to slow, a gust of mistrust blowing through it. "*Are* you me?… Do I sound like that?" it asked itself again.

"Giraffe!" resounded the voice, abruptly. Next it was more of a timid question, "Giraffe?" "John," John told the voice, sternly cutting through its giraffe curses and questions, "it's me – Cameron – you know me as Cameron – that used to be my name – but now it's John. My name's changed but that's not important. Do you understand?… What's all this talk about giraffes and whether I'm me or you, or you're you or me?"

has one of us gone crazy

"Cameron…" it said out loud to itself, "John…" comparing the sounds of the names. "When did I know you as Cameron? *I've* never been called Cameron… I don't think… at least not yet…" "It's me, your neighbour, Cameron. We talked a few days ago through this wall – just like this – about…" What they'd actually talked about wasn't immediately forthcoming, "… about the food, and living here, and things like that – oh and that recording, remember?" "Hmmm," the voice was disappointed.

"So, you're not me?" it repeated, "I'm John," it added, obligingly. "No," it continued, muttering, "I didn't think I sounded like that." Forgetting the bizarre context, John felt a passing insecurity about his own voice.

As he heard himself reassuring the voice, he was certain of its owner's madness, "No, I'm not you. I'm me." "Then why did you say you *were* me?" it retorted, hurt and confused, "You don't even sound like me!" "I didn't!" reacted John, losing his patience, "And anyway what do you mean, 'I'm not you'? Of course I'm not you: I'm me! I'm me and you're you: we're two separate people!"

In a spell of quiet that followed, John recalled, "Yes, I did tell you I was John just now. My name used to be Cameron, or at least I thought it was Cameron, but now it's John. (I've since found out it's John – my name that is.) But," he added hastily, "it's just a coincidence," though he wondered at it himself, "it just so happens we share the same name – it's a very common name." He'd now given up treating his interlocutor as a sane person, "But we are *not* the same person, that's the main thing." He let the conclusion sink in.

"So you've not already agreed to help me, have you?" the voice came through with a hint of petulant accusation. "No… sorry, I don't follow you?… How can I help you?" John responded. Silence returned alone through the wall. "Ah but maybe you can help then!?" It seemed a new idea had been struck upon. "How?" replied John, curtly.

he may be insane but maybe he can still tell me something

Phrased this way, the insight unwittingly invited along some guilt to be shaken off. "And you'll help yourself too," the voice had rambled on, "if it works, we can both escape!" "Escape?" repeated John to himself. The voice had snagged his curiosity and now had his complete attention.

"Yes, let me explain: I'm trying to build a time machine but I think I need another person's help to do it."

a time machine?

The voice waited for John's permission to continue. John was silent. His spirits, having rapidly risen high when escape was mentioned, now fell sharply.

what sort of company am I in keeping with in this place

Although turned idle, John's curiosity was still there, equal to the boredom he often felt alone. "Right, and so how will you build this time machine?" he asked. "I haven't the first clue" shot back the voice, eager to resume the conversation. "Oh... well, I'm sorry, but I don't either. So I don't think I can help you," he told the voice.

"Ah, well, *I as such* haven't the first clue but my future-self does, and I've arranged to meet him here, in this exact time and place. He'll then tell me how to build one, or more likely give me one ready-made, and I can escape! – *We* can escape!" it corrected itself. "So… your future-self will give you a time machine?" "Exactly." "But how does he have one? How does he know how to build one?" John asked. "Precisely, yes: because he'll be me in the future (by definition). So he would've already been told, in the past, how to build one (when he was me stuck in here)… So it does mean I'll have to return here myself, at some point in my lifetime (as my future-self), to pass on the instructions or a second machine to me now… but after that my debt will be paid off, so to speak – I'll be free from here – and I'll have my very own time machine!"

John wondered at the madman's logic. "So, why are you still here then?" he asked. Remembering, "Why do you need my help?" "Well, it hasn't worked."

no kidding

He couldn't state exactly why though. The voice went on, "I think maybe it's because it's impossible to meet one's self. That's where you come in. By all four of us agreeing to set up a relay of communication, none of us has to meet his future- or past-self. Your future-self can rescue me and mine can rescue you." "How will they do that when we're locked up in here?" asked John. "Oh think about it: besides having a time machine, they'll have access to all kinds of future technology, so it will be easy."

"I'm sorry", John told the voice, "but I'm not interested. Why don't you have your future-self ask someone in the future to help?" "What?" It was flustered. "No, I'm sure I've tried that but it doesn't work. Look, I know I said I didn't have a clue before, but once we're successful we'll know exactly how to build the machine – they'll give us the instructions. We'll know exactly what we're doing. Then we just have to pass them back on. Please!" it pleaded. "Sorry," John repeated. "Just try!" the voice begged, "In the name of scientific experiment."

why not

The question appeared before him. "OK, fine. But — so what do I have to do?" "Fantastic!" said the voice, ecstatically. "OK, we need to agree on a signal. You need to remember where you are, and keep track of how much time passes before I enter your cell. I don't know how much of the work we can leave to them." "Before you enter my cell?" "Yes: my future-self. So, you make the signal, and I'll come into your cell and rescue you. And remember to keep track of how much time passes between making the signal and me entering the cell. We're doing this now, OK? It's exciting, isn't it? Are you ready?" "OK?… "

   "So the signal: I suggest you shout something in a low-pitched voice. (Lower frequencies travel better through thick materials like steel.) How about 'giraffe', actually no, no, that's been done – well, sort of – something brand new – 'forest fruits'?" "'Forest fruits'?" "Yes. Shout 'forest fruits', repeatedly, in low pitches, until I find you. Don't worry, it shouldn't take long. And if I don't reply 'bread' before I enter, then you know something's not right. OK? Oh, and my future-self will tell you the code words for my rescue and escape. I'll decide them now."

John was having second thoughts. "I'm not sure about this any more," he admitted, "It won't work. I'm sorry, but trust me: it won't work." "Not if you don't try!" The voice was startled. "You're not serious? Now come on, you've already agreed. You have any better ideas? Please *try*. We could both *escape*! Imagine that. Try at least, please." "Yes, yes, OK. I'll try just to see if it works, but if it doesn't, I'm stopping." "Good, excellent!" said the voice, happy again, "Thank you! OK, so let's do it. I'll stay silent now and cover my ears. Because it's important I don't interact with my future-self, remember? In your own time: 'forest fruits', remember, and 'bread' is the reply."

Encouraged by indifference and a lack of embarrassment, John stood up, walked to the centre of his cell, and let 'forest fruits' rebound around the walls in a low pitch. For good measure, he did this a few times rhythmically. Soon he succumbed to throwing the words out in varied shouts as the feeling took him.

so what if Lucy thinks I'm mad! it's better than being bored anyway

He took a break and sat on the toilet, a little breathless.

this is actually surprisingly enjoyable

He leant back, thinking about his mad neighbour's idea.

now how do I know it can't work

As he was busying his brain, his eyes fell on the door.

what if did work, it would be a miracle if it did… in theory, I suppose your future-self could tell you anything you wanted to know… so long as you then passed the information on yourself later… you'd become omniscient and omnipotent… God… all from a ridiculous logical loophole… everything from nothing

There was a sound outside. John sat up startled. The door was opening and someone was entering.

no one said bread… should I say bread

A cyan uniform appeared. It was just Lucy.

no passwords out after all

Sobering, belated embarrassment ebbed over his body. He dreaded the sudden vision of a large gift of wild berries swinging in behind Lucy.

10 INTRUDER

The moon must've been covered by clouds. The night before faint shards of luminescence had lit the floor a pale grey. However, tonight the whole cell was cast in nothing but the dark.

there's someone else in my cell

John's breathing instinctively constricted. He lay frozen to his bed and cast his ears out into the surrounding black air. The intruder was in the corner opposite the door.

how did they get in

He hadn't sensed the door open or close.
 A rustling was coming from the corner.

what are they doing

He wanted to look in the direction of the sounds, but daren't shift his body. The rustling grew louder.

they're looking for something

Statue-like, John turned onto his side to face the room. His eyes had now adjusted more to the murky surroundings. Yet searching into the corner, his expanding pupils were met only with a consuming blackness.

Hearing the scratching of metal on concrete, he felt his heart stop.

the grenade

From within the depths of shadow, the intruder's gaze had met his own. A figure had the grenade in hand.

Outside dense clouds were gently weakened by a breeze, and a slender strip of moonlight struck a man's face. He was standing in the middle of the room now. Icy air sharply seized the walls of John's lungs. Standing before him was his very self. He was stood staring right back at him, lying on the bed.

It was too much to process and he didn't have time to think. His likeness held up the grenade in the light. His other hand ceremoniously approached the ring pull. He already appeared oblivious to John watching from the bed, unable to speak. He wanted to shout at him: 'You're crazy! Stop! What are you doing!?' The sticky dryness of his throat caught him. The man's index finger had slipped through the ring pull. It tightened firmly around the thin strip of metal.

John leapt from the bed at his assailant. As he knocked the man to the floor, he heard a satisfying click. The grenade bounced on the floor towards the bed. From beneath, smiling spitefully at him, the man displayed the ring pull in his fingers. His expression changed: in quick transition, next going from shameful regret to utter despair. With a look of profound apology, he tried to tell him something. It was too late.

John fell out of bed in an icy sweat, gulping in the fresh air. He stumbled to the door, knocking into it, immediately kicking and thumping at the steel, screaming, "Help! Lucy! Intruder! Doctor! The grenade! Cameron-John! Now! Open the door now! It's about to explode!" His raving eyes darted back behind him.

Moonlight steadily streamed through the bars, insensible to his yelling.

… no one there…

He looked into the corner to the right of the toilet. There he saw the patchy silhouette of the grenade. With an effort, he inhaled deeply, trying to steady the pace of his breathing. His chest felt as if it might crack. He sleeked sweaty threads of hair back off his damp forehead. "It was just a dream… a bad dream… I'm safe… I'm still alive."

this is my real life and that wasn't

"That wasn't… That wasn't real," he muttered. He tried to pace his breathing with his steps, walking up and down through the shadows in front of his bed. Each time a heel came up and the ball of the other foot pressed down, he felt the clinical coldness beneath supporting his weight. Nerves still weren't completely settled.

On each walk back towards the steel toilet, John stopped to look at the grenade. He could see its outline more clearly now. He walked towards it, bent down, and picked it up. He was fondling it, until his fingers found the ring pull still attached. His chest rose and then his lungs emptied, as he breathed out audibly in relief.

it was just a horrible dream

Coming to, he realised the slender cold object in the crease of a strong finger was the ring pull.

the same one in my nightmare

He felt the sudden impulse to yank it out. Something travelled slowly yet with gathering speed: down from his brain; past his neck and into his shoulders; to his triceps; his forearms; into his wrists — in a spasm, he dropped the object and shuddered.

The grenade hit hardness in the grey below and his stomach leapt up.

the knock could set it off!

Panicking, John half-crouched and broke into a fresh sweat, pressing the air around him with outstretched palms as if to soothe it from combustion. Nothing happened, besides rolling metallic sounds behind him. Turning, he found the grenade waiting innocently off-centre on the steel floor. With his right foot, he carefully brushed it towards the steel table in the corner. After this, he had walked back to his bed, got in and pulled the sheets over him. Exhausted, he fell asleep.

11 TERROR

John was bathing in grey light. His mind soaked in the overcast sky's cloudy currents, the back of his head on a pillow.

Abruptly to the side landed the heavy sound of footfall. Rolling his head to the right, his eyes glimpsed solid green-blue movements in the slender rectangular spaces between the bars of his window. He sat up quickly, his left knee pointed to the ceiling with his right leg crossed underneath. Crouching down to face him between the bars was Lucy.

"Don't mind me," she explained from within her grey-walled cuboid, "I'm just here to take some measurements." John stood up on the bed and leant forwards, "How did you get there? What are you doing?" "Taking measurements," Lucy repeated patiently. "What measurements? Why?" "Oh, it's nothing really. I'll be gone in a moment," she replied, already busy in the overcast light with her work.

John gripped the bars, watching her. He was about to press more with his inquiry, but Lucy went on unprovoked, "This is going to be blocked up for you. We're getting a new metal sheet to cover it up. You'll be warmer." "Blocked up?" echoed John, before responding, "But wait a minute, I don't want it blocked up. It's fine as it is." "That's right, the window's going to be blocked up for you," repeated Lucy. "But I like having a window there. I'm not cold." Lucy didn't seem to hear. "Couldn't we keep the window there?" John pleaded. As he said this, he'd tried to reach out to touch her arm. However, due to her current position and the narrow gaps, he only achieved a pathetic pawing motion. "Sorry," said Lucy, conclusively. She turned to the side and hoisted herself out.

John's eyes tried to follow, but he was thwarted once again by the uncaring grey wall.

I know the sky is just a little farther up, just once!

He craned his neck back, as he'd done before. Striking his least favourite steel bar with his palm, he slumped back onto his sheets. The alcove behind the bars was empty once again, just as it had always been. Yet Lucy had just been there, and they'd just talked. He laughed at this, before thumping the wall with the soft side portion of a fist.

The light had continued to dim when Lucy's clinking heralds hurried through the lock to John's ears, which were by the wall opposite the bed. It wasn't time for dinner yet, and when Lucy entered, she wasn't holding a tray. With the door pressed shut, she marched over to the bed. Still standing, she took off her shoes to reveal two well-formed feet. John stood watching from the corner opposite the door. When she turned back to him, she was already stood on the bed, "You don't mind, do you? I'm just here to take some more measurements." Turning away, the periphery of the window now confined her attention.

John wandered into the centre of the white floor. "Actually, I do mind," he explained, "I don't want you to block up my window. I don't understand why you're doing it? I won't get any fresh air. And it'll stop any natural light from coming in." Lucy stopped what she was doing and turned to look down at him. She crouched down, just beneath the lines of words he'd cast up to her. "The temperature in here's already just fine – just perfect as it is!" he tagged on, appeasingly. He watched as Lucy's gaze drifted to his right where he'd just been standing. He didn't have her attention.

Her eyes surveyed the emptiness of the white corner. Stepping down, she walked up to him. Standing by his side, she crouched to look up at the window.

she's continuing with her measuring

Lucy straightened up and walked towards the left of the bed and window, where the table was fixed. John's pupils scurried ahead on her path for at its end was the grenade.

I moved it back there after my dream last night

Her body blocked his view as she knelt beneath the table. She emerged holding the retrieved weighty black and red object.

Lucy glided back to the centre of the white floor. John took a step back. With the grenade left neatly on the floor, Lucy stood up. As their eyes met, her deft hand steadied the space between them, requesting permission to speak first. She slowly walked back, not relinquishing the permission she'd obtained, and sat on the bed.

"Do you believe in an afterlife?" John was asked. He was accustomed to Lucy's strange inquiries by now. "No," he replied, waiting for the next question. A silence developed and Lucy's eyebrows rose receptively at it. She leaned back into her wrists. "Well, do you?" he reciprocated. "Of course," replied Lucy, "At least, that is," she corrected herself, "if there wasn't an afterlife, then life would be absurd. Therefore, there is one."

Stood there across from her, John realised they were now having a discussion. "It's sound logic," Lucy appealed to a sceptical mien. "Yes, it's sound logic," John replied irritably, keen to dismiss the eccentric conversation. If he was going to be confronted, it would be with actions, not silly word games.

Ignoring Lucy's presence, he bent down and picked out the black and red object from the white steel beneath. Although his mind was occupied with Lucy's stare, he felt relatively relaxed as he walked the grenade over to the left of her. He nested it back in its place, underneath the table. Then he took his own place, back in the centre of the cell. The action completed, he stood facing Lucy.

The power of the rebel gripped his veins. All he needed now was a layer of time to bury the act. In control, he took up the debate again. "Yes, it's sound logic," he replied, "But what if life is absurd?" Lucy spoke slowly, "Well… yes… that's precisely the question, I suppose." He'd been anticipated.

With unnerving confidence, she stood up, "Maybe life *is* absurd." Lucy walked to the place under the table and crouched down. Straightening back up, she walked back across the steel whiteness with the grenade in hand. "But then if life is absurd…" At the centre of the cell, she placed the object in careful contrast with the floor, "then…" Moving her open palm casually to the side, the grenade presented itself.

The moment had lingered grotesquely before she'd quietly raised herself up. "But of course, you're the one who suggested it was," she added, with a teasing smile, "Well, either way…" She broke off, lost in a thought before resurfacing with it, "I like to imagine the afterlife as bright, fresh and free." John was eyed by her in a naturally cold silence. She turned her back on him and stepped back up onto the bed. Once more, she was absorbed by the dimensions of the window.

John felt something like a dripping in his heart, one which couldn't be fully absorbed. A ghastly new notion of Lucy began to congeal there, as sinister as the interaction just passed.

He bent down to pick up the metallic object resting at his feet. Still examining the window and surrounding wall, Lucy took to talking again, "You've never been bothered about the lack of space before." She'd caught him stood still, grenade in hand. He remained where he was, listening, "So I don't understand why you're bothered about it now?" He'd forgotten that he'd picked the grenade up to move it back to its safe place. "Come to think of it, given you don't mind your lack of space here, why mind a lack of *time*?"

Familiar with Lucy's lines of reasoning, he quickly comprehended her approach. "Science tells us it's incorrect to think of them as separate. In fact, perhaps the Universe is like a book: beginning, middle and end already written; time flows as we read it but that's just an illusion. Such is life…

"Well, in any case – time or space – our lots of both are finite. Therefore, after a certain point, any amount of either is much the same. Our stories all take place somewhere and end some day!"

so cruel, yes very subtle Lucy, how basic do you think I am

He was disgusted. "I suppose what's more important is *quality*… I am sorry, you know, about you no longer having your window." As she made the apology, she turned back to him.

Having done so, her subsequent expression set increate ideas in motion. She was frightened. Her casual talk had stopped, condensing into paleness. The two both looked down at the grenade in John's hand.

John gleefully seized the revenge on offer. "So what you're saying, Lucy, is we should kill ourselves?" "What? No, no, I didn't say that — where did you get that from?" Although her words were irritating, her anxious tone was compensation. John felt freer. "Or at least you wouldn't be bothered if it all ended now? Time is space and they're both finite and all that. *Science* tells us so. Right?" "No — I don't understand? What's that got to —" "Shut up! It's a rhetorical question, you moron! I'm not asking you what you told me: I'm *telling* you… And let's see how you feel about it now. You've done you're talking, and now I'll do mine. So shut up!"

Lucy's face was empty, and she replied in an empty murmur, "Yes, I'm listening." Necessity pulled her slowly down to the bed, from where the space of floor between them took her fallen eyes. John resumed with the same energy, "That's what you said, don't deny it – but no, you *want* it to all end now, don't you? Life is absurd after all – so why go on with it? That's what you think, and you want me persuaded of it too." His crazed anger was now directed at himself for having let her words get to him. The more he heard the effects of rage in his voice, the more enraged he became. He lowered himself calmly to see her face more clearly, "Well congratulations, you have persuaded me! So why don't we end it all *together*? *Now.* The two of us. No time like the present!"

Lucy's large wet eyes silently rose and poured into his. Her look confirmed something: at some lost primal moment, John was no longer merely ranting back to Lucy her suggestions; he'd become possessed by the twisted meaning of his words. But he couldn't stop now, "Or wait – but you *deny* life is absurd? And that's the only alternative. But that's because there's an afterlife – where everything's obviously better. So why not go there now? It'll be great there. Lots of fresh air and open windows… with no bitches to come in and block them up whilst casually suggesting that you kill yourself!"

Her eyes had no effect on him. No sympathy nor human feeling was aroused, and he felt a sadistic pleasure at the power this gave him. The drunken power devolved into something sicker, and its repulsiveness seduced him. The knowledge his own body might be made the nameless cause of Suffering fevered his mind. All he need do, in the wake of an instant, was will it, just once. The ground beneath his feet felt desperate. "You're trembling," Lucy blurted out. But before the observation was finished, with a snap, the red ring pull was yanked out.

Time grew thick: it was too thick to move. John and Lucy witnessed each other transfixed. Only together could their minds wade through, though with burdensome language left behind. The sick power abandoned John. He'd been used. The cost would be Lucy's life and his own. Frames of the large imploring female eyes before him stacked up in the now in a fresh reel of memory.

why am I me and not her

His heart broke open, and love and apology poured out towards her.

but it can't carry her away

It was the timeless scene of a diorama with Death the only visitor. There the pair existed, like words on a page unchanging, trapped by their final description.

* * *

Lucy stood up; she took a step forward. Her expression changed, separating her from the man and the situation. She was watching him, ambivalently, and then with pleasure. He suddenly felt like an actor who'd forgotten his lines. "It would've gone off by now," she said softly.

would've…

Lucy had turned and was walking away to his left.

has it not gone off, are we dead at the start of our afterlives

Her cyan back contrasted with the white section of wall between the door and fountain. On the area of floor below was the grenade.

it's about to explode!

The idea pounced on him. Yet Lucy's behaviour was protecting him. He finally understood the meaning of her first words.

it would've gone off by now, it would have… *so it hasn't… and it's not* going to?

The grenade was different. It had lost its dangerous vivid red and was now just a dead black, like a lifeless spider curled up out of harm's way.
She had picked it up. She was walking back, with him in her path. He took a step back as she passed closely in front of him.

I can move… I still have a body… a whole *body*

Her eyes slanted back towards him, aimed at his feet. At his heel to the right was a piece of red metal.

that's longer than it should be

Lucy wanted this too. He took another step back, this time to the left. She stood up to face him with both objects in her hand.

parts of the same object

Lucy laughed naturally. But it was an inhuman laugh, and it was pitched at him. "So you wanted to bring me into this? Tried to kill us both?" The laugh had cleared a path for speech. "Tried to kill *me*!?" Beneath the smooth skin of her face, muscles contorted demonically. Her eyes were no longer windows; everything had risen to the surface. But only for a flash.

Her usual demeanour returned professionally, "The grenade is deactivated whenever others are in the room," she explained.

deactivated

An answer had been given and it contained others. However, for John, the context was blurred. If he'd been tricked, he hadn't processed the possibility.

The source of Lucy's sudden calm was a deadly coldness. Behind her eyes, in the frost, John saw a demon set on him.

"But it's OK," she proceeded, advancing towards him, "I'll get it reset for you." She waved the two parts together at him in either hand, black and red, seeking to break his daze. He stumbled back and his shoulders found the hard steel wall.

She stayed put, watching her human thing from where she was and enjoying their roles. "Well, you've done it once now." She moved. John's shoulders ran in a smooth arc along the wall, away from the door to his left and down towards the corner to his right. He landed slumped, facing the looming steel of the toilet's side. He only experienced her voice as she called to him from the door, "You've done it once. It shows you can do it. You've done it once, so you can do it again. I'll just get this reset for you." Metal slamming shut echoed everywhere.

12   AMELIA

There was a knock at the door. As he had been since he could remember, John was lying in bed. From where his head was framed in sheets, he spied the entrance of a white coat.

that psychiatrist…

but not John, Dr Cameron, I'm John and that's Dr Cameron… he's come to study my mind… but he can only ever know it from the outside… in a moment we'll be talking about something

Dr Cameron was in the centre of the cell. He was being observed. "Hello, John," said the white-coated torso.

was that a question, what should I say back… maybe I could just keep silent

He sat up slowly, wrapped in his sheets. His eyes climbed up the white coat to its top, "Yes, hello," he replied.

"I've come to talk with you," Dr Cameron was expressionless, "about an incident." He paused, waiting. "I've already talked with Lucy and now I've come to speak with you too." "Yes?" said John, not intending to make the word a question. "Maybe you can talk first," suggested Dr Cameron. "About what?" "The incident," the words arrived patiently. "Yes, the incident." It was foggy where he wanted to recall connections or language, but he sensed this was an opportunity.

a personal interview with Dr Cameron about recent events

He sat groping for what he thought he wanted to say.

"Lucy's trying to kill me," came out. He stared at Dr Cameron. Dr Cameron looked back at him. Each waited for the other. "Go on," prompted Dr Cameron, attentively. Abhorrent confusion bolstered John's stare. "This is your time to talk," Dr Cameron explained in response, "I'm listening. I've listened to Lucy and now I'm going to listen to you." John's fixed stare, like a lighthouse beacon, swept up and down the man before him. It completed its journey to be reflected off the psychiatrist's glasses.

"But that's it! What more is there to say? *Lucy is trying to kill me!*" The psychiatrist spoke: "Please can you tell me, what exactly did Lucy do?" "It's not what she did, it's the things she says. But what does that matter?" He was standing up now. "*She is trying to kill me.*" He was sure he'd repeated this already now; it was as though his supply of words for the statement were all duds. "Nobody is trying to kill you," assured the white-coated man.

"And what about the grenade!?" shot back John, "It's *not* just her words: it's her actions. There's going to be another grenade put back in here, isn't there?" "Ms Marshvale is only doing her job. As am I. Trust us, please. Trust me. Trust her." John slumped back onto the bed, cradled by his wrap of white sheets. A clumsy rubber sole squeaking on marble was stuck in his head.

"I want to see my wife." That rarer species of thought born fresh on the tongue, it was a surprise to both pairs of ears present. Dr Cameron crouched down, the white steel expanse now level between the two men. His expression confirmed what John already knew, "I have a wife, don't I? I knew it! I want to see her." "There's a reason you can't remember your past, John. It's best to keep it that way. Try not to remember your past, OK?"

John jumped up. He threw the screwed-up weight of sheets on the bed with a violent thud. The psychiatrist quickly stood up with him but stayed where he was. "I want to see my wife!" shouted John. He took a step forwards. "Remember how you felt, after the incident that happened recently?" Dr Cameron asked him, "You didn't feel good afterwards, did you? And even now, I know, you don't feel yourself."

He quickly examined what was before him. "Let's not have another incident before your wife visits," he continued. "Before my wife visits?" John caught hold of the promise tightly. "Yes, yes," Dr Cameron stepped towards him and put his hand on his shoulder. Two different expressions met each other, "I'll arrange it for you." He left.

John was alone again, sitting. He'd dreamt of his wife often. He'd given up wondering if any of the dreams might also be memories, or what percentage of reality they contained. It almost didn't matter. Whatever they were, they were pleasant and soft, though admittedly in part because the details were fuzzy. Awaiting her visit, he was preparing for the strange gap between expectation and reality.

He was excited. Ahead to his left from the bed, he looked over to the door. At some moment soon, the person he'd fallen in love with, was in love with and would fall in love with again, would walk into the room through that white rectangle. Even if his life ended here, he would have seen her first. They would have met again. And that fact would be eternally true, long after they'd both vanished.

I hope she can give me some answers.

A voice atomised fragrantly in his heart and was carried into his blood. It was calling his name, beckoning him.

John

It was a female voice.

it's her

A soft knocking came from somewhere. John stood up. The knocking repeated. He looked over to the door. Slowly his feet moved towards the sound, emotions suspended. "John?" The greeting found its way timidly into the cell.

the same voice as just now!

He was quickly at the white steel of the door. He responded, with the same soft knocking he'd been sent, "Hello?" he whispered onto the white metal. "Hello? John, it's me," said the female voice. "Hello, yes, I know you've come to see me. Come in," he told her, excitedly. "I'm sorry but I can't. It's lucky that they've let us talk at all." Sadness gently touched him, "I'm sorry too – for all this." "I love you," her own voice replied. "I love you," he added his testimony to hers. They shared a moment of quietness.

John's questions emerged, "Why am I here? What's going on?" There was no reply. "Hello?" "Yes, I'm here. But let's not talk about it?" she asked. "OK," he told her, assuringly, "But you know I've lost my memory?" "Yes." "I thought my name was *Cameron* when I first woke up here! Imagine that? But that's the name of the psychiatrist in charge here. Well, his surname: Dr Cameron. But now I know my name's John. It was nice hearing you say my name just now. I mean in *your* voice but *my* name." He stopped to think, unsuccessfully. "What's—" He cut himself off, embarrassed. "My name's Amelia," she told him. "Amelia," he echoed back to them both, "Yes, I think maybe I knew that… I'm sorry but there's some things I just haven't been able to remember."

Amelia waited for him to go on, "I work in the Law Bureau, don't I? And we live in a ground-floor apartment which leads out to a courtyard garden… and there are flowers everywhere." "Yes, yes," she answered, choking on a laugh. She could indulge them both now, if only a little, "You work in law, and we live in a ground-floor apartment. And it's especially beautiful in the summer when all the flowers are in bloom. Well, *I* think so anyway – you've always preferred the autumn." "And you like to sketch, don't you?" he weaved in, eager to take them deeper into reminiscence. "Yes, I like to sketch." "You always used to sketch in the mornings when I left early to walk to work. And we kissed goodbye at the door, after having breakfast together." "Yes," she confirmed, but her voice was empty this time. "And I always used to walk to work, and I never liked taking the train."

A slow sob haunted his ears. "Amelia? I'm sorry. What did I say? Please don't cry. I'm sorry, I didn't mean to say that." "No, it's nothing," said a wet voice, just managing to soak through the steel, "Don't be sorry... but I am – I have to go. I never imagined we'd be able to talk about so much... but I'm glad we have. Take this." A sheet of folded paper poked through at the side of the door. John gripped it. He felt her gentle fingers on the other side release. "Goodbye," she said, in a loud whisper.

He knew she was gone.

I'll never see her again

He stayed by the door. Reminded of eternity, he let his back slide down its surface to the floor where he hunched over. He curled up at the door's base, facing the corner towards where it opened. With the paper pressed between his palms, he fell asleep.

John had postponed his wife's last communication
with him. However, now, sat on his bed in afternoon
light, he succumbed. He unfolded the paper.
Through the paper's whiteness, his eyes had long
before already caressed the pattern of dark ink. He
found what he'd been expecting: a poem. He looked
at it like a painting first, before slowly reading.

Another world, the tides tweaked a fraction,
The possible swells to a different form,
Amid a lost place, we're here together,
Souls settled where the fine present's not torn,

But it's dummies owning ever lone stars,
Dead worlds lit only with envy charged through,
Though us, we're not the same pair without us,
Disjointed and left forsaken as two,

Not in a category past remote,
Possibly possible, the void's just time,
Eternity can't now always exist
Waiting to witness a fictional chime.

Hope dances on peaks of future and mist,
Her incense entangles even when shunned,
Abandoning the mountain sun to heal burns
Despair in chasms is met with unarmed,

A hopeless scent makes the demons deadly,
Onward they trail, their steady gaze too,
A shadow awaits its flesh lurking near,
All steps a mere tracing in empty hue,

AMELIA

Back by a ridge, stumbles hope at each turn,
Twilight corners with murmurs of maybe,
Come for a beating but never to die,
Beautiful, nagging, beggar–like lady.

Breathing fresh air but broad waters surround,
Thick sea waves where leaping eyes tumble,
I tread water, feel the depths that plunge down,
Still getting tired refusing to drown.

13 REVENGE

Let's say you do make it out," Lucy had continued.
As she'd started again, her speech took on an
unnaturally strange rhythm, "And then, climb the
highest mountain you can find – with the cloudy
skies now below you… the sun there would still be
the same as yesterday's, and the same as
tomorrow's… when you're gone."

Long afterwards, the awkwardly connected images
troubled him, even now with his mind buried
beneath his pillow. Unable to translate the metaphor,
he was nonetheless fluent in its language and sort
comfort.

the view would still be worth it

On a dim edge of dreams, despair hissed.

or would've been

None of the counters in his wearied head suited him,
and he surrendered to black sleep.

John was starting to wake, when the resonance of shutting marked itself the official start of reality that day. He looked over to the door. On the table, steam rose from breakfast. He ignored his breakfast as food, and wondered if Lucy had just been in the cell.

I'd rather not think about her

He boldly cast her out.

I'd rather think about Amelia

His thoughts on Amelia refrained from constructing possible futures; at the same time, he was incapable of accepting there may be none.

He shifted onto his front. Leaning over the edge of the thin sheeted mattress, he picked up the poem which he'd laid neatly behind the head of the bed. As he sat up, the heat of the fresh coffee on the table caught his attention. He walked over and took the coffee cup back to bed, the poem in his other hand. Sat against the wall and back in the warmth of his sheets, he was soon settled into both coffee and poem.

It was the handwritten letters that most entranced him: their ink and spacing all connected physically with Amelia, and now in his hands, with him. One of his favourite parts of the poem was a smudge. Of course, he also read it as it should be. However, whereas there'd always be time to enjoy or attend to the meaning of the words, as he'd soon have them learnt by heart, in the future the precious original might be lost.

When he delicately returned the paper to its remote place, his coffee had long cooled inside him. He paced his cell, a path now so familiar that with smooth strides he could trample with ease Time itself. Now and then, he stopped in the centre and turned to the window. He rejoiced that it was still there.

whether it'll be blocked up in the future it isn't now

He enjoyed the light as it cast itself through his body in refreshing waves. The air was fresh too and he seemed peaceful, an inhabitant of the luxurious present. At least the grenade was no longer in the cell; in those rare moments, nor was its absence.

Breakfast sat dejected on the table, and John's stomach now wanted lunch. He sat on the bed wondering about the future when his ear drums jingled. Familiar keys engaged with a lock. The door was opening, and Lucy walked in. Like a ghost, she performed her cyclic routine. His lunch was on the tray.

"Good afternoon, John," she looked over at him but was met by blankness. Part of him wanted to ask if she'd been avoiding him. However, most of him was only ready to first listen to speech before producing it. She proceeded in a line to the table with lunch.

As he heard Lucy set the tray down, a black speck to his right buzzed into his field of vision. He turned to look up. Stationed at the table, Lucy was looking down at him. "I won't be visiting any more," she explained at him. Her hand lay on something. "It would detract from covering the window," her face continued. There was a webbed blackness in between the fingers of the hand rested on the tray. "But I'll leave you with this," she announced. She held up her hand and the black parts beneath transformed into an object. When she moved it before her for display, a red streak threaded through space beyond a cyan backdrop.

"But this isn't the same grenade," she explained, setting it back on the tray. She studied John. His mind was in hibernation. She marched over and crouched down before him. "*This isn't the same grenade,*" she repeated. It was just the two of them.

if no one listens to her then her words are meaningless

He stared out. "The first grenade was a fake!" She took his jaw in her hands to direct a lost stare at her. "But this one's real! *I* replaced it with a real one," she told her one-man audience. "I'm a mother, John. I have a life and a family. And if left to you, it would've been taken from me."

Lucy released her hold and walked back to the door. Her movements paid cautious attention to the different distances constituting the situation. She unlocked the door. Instead of opening it, she looked back. "According to the rules, this isn't allowed," she called to him, "But did it ever occur to you that I can break the rules?" He didn't react. "No need to thank me for lunch. The opportunity to ruin my life with yours is gone now, but you still have the power to ruin Amelia's." She gestured towards the table: "when you can find the time, all you need is there."

John raised his stare to her and stood up with it. He walked towards the table with sudden speed. She quickly opened the door. As he arrived at the table, the door shut and Lucy had disappeared.

John was left to look at the contents on the tray. He resolved to sit down and eat lunch.

that's my plan so far and I'll stick to it, have lunch, I can decide what to do next after

The grenade sat like a free toy with his meal. He prepared himself. He quickly picked it up, shivering at a rush of blurred images that flowed through his body.

done

He'd set it down under the table, out of the way. He'd moved it like that once and he could do it again.

Without noticing what lunch was, John's fork was being raised to his mouth. He inserted the food. As he chewed, he tasted images of Lucy and he spat it out. With a sudden craving, he picked up the tray and turned around. He hurled it wrathfully at the wall by the door, watching its contents fly on ahead. With spiteful satisfaction, he witnessed the array of carefully prepared substances collide with a white metallic canvas.

Lucy

Time had strode on towards evening. Spurred on by his excess of purposeless energy, John had exercised his body by pacing the cell. As he did so, his mind loosely caught the essence of his lot's latest development.

However, now, lying on the bed, his convictions were lost in the shadowy ceiling above. It had darkened outside, and the weather had changed.

As he looked over to the door where the mess of food and cutlery lay, the light in the cell switched on. His hunger hadn't yet expanded to consume the rejected food in the corner, but he wondered about dinner.

Lucy isn't coming back, does that mean I won't be given any more food, or will someone else give me my food, perhaps Dr Cameron?

The last possibility seemed the most reasonable conjecture, though also the most hopeful.

He looked up at his window. The black hole there reminded him of his stomach. He sat up. Planting his feet on the floor, he observed the wall opposite. He wasn't tired.

I'm hungry, *not tired, I could have another look at the poem? no it's better to ration it*

Suddenly, the light cut out. Roaming dark devoured the room. Immediately, the door opened, and a burly figure entered. "Stay where you are," a large male voice commanded. John darted to the corner behind the head of his bed, diagonally opposite the door. "I said stay where you are!" boomed the voice. John's breathing lied of a marathon distance between where he'd just sat and now currently hid.

"We're here to give you your dinner," announced the dark cell. The steps of the figure left a trail across the wall opposite, from the door to the table. John's hand drifted through the blackness to the precious sheet of paper laid by the head of his bed. Having a grip of the poem, he slowly pulled it back against a dark tide.

Based on the shading of the corner, the inward-opening door was ajar. Strange sounds were congregated there with large movements, as if the door itself had come to life.

he'd said we're *here*

The steps which had travelled to the table collected themselves back at the entrance. The door opened in a little wider, and two hefty shadows exited.

Like magic, the light switched back on. John cautiously stood up. He ranged into the middle of the room, looking around. His advance took him to the door. An area of floor and wall shined wet. The mess was gone. He turned to walk over to the table.

dinner!

On a plate on the tray was pasta in a thin sauce.

He ate greedily, only stopping once to glug water at the fountain. His stomach gradually grew heavy. After dinner, he wanted to walk and think. However, layers of sleep came quickly to weigh him down. Falling into bed, he soon lost his body in it.

14 CEREMONY

Something forming into an ever-heavier stone slab seemed to press down flat on John's body, and then his body was gone. However, he was still lucid; he knew he'd just been sleeping. As he wondered where he was, shapes and colours emerged.

Around him was a small silently lit room, which centred on a bare rectangular table set with four surrounding empty wooden chairs. John took up one of the chairs and sat down. He was waiting for someone to appear in the chair facing him. The buzz of people dining flooded into the barren space, and an alternative atmosphere was offered, before the singular click of a door shutting sealed it off.

A face appeared across the table. Below the large forehead, and beneath silky eyebrows, were displayed a pair of dead-animal eyes. The face was vacantly consuming his own. John felt hollow.

"Well?" asked the Director General, "I understand you have questions for me? That's why we're both here." He waited, watching. "As you know, this is all in your head…" He gave John time to realise it. "Yes," resumed the Director, clarifying the fact, "Nonetheless, you can still ask me your questions and I can do my best to answer."

"I want the truth about why I'm here," announced John. "OK," replied the Director, "but it might take some time. Let's start on our meal while I explain." He gestured to a plate in front of John. On it was soft dark meat. The Director had picked up a sharp knife and fork, and held them casually at the sides of his plate.

"There *is* a reason, of course. You're here, or rather *there* (in the cell) if you prefer," he began, "on charges of suspected irrationality." He cut away some of the fleshy meat and raised it to his mouth. As it passed in, it brushed the wet sides of his lips. "Are you not hungry?" John was asked. The Director had already gulped down the bolus, barely having had to chew. "What meat is this?" John asked. The Director studied the question in the space between them. "You see, this is an example, I think," he replied, "Did you not hear what I just told you? I just told you why you're here…

"It's petite meat. Why aren't you eating it?" "I don't like it." "Exactly. You say that and yet you like the taste and texture. Is it the morality of it you don't like? I understand this is a reasonable consideration. However, there's no suffering involved in the production of this meat, whereas there is in cases of other types of meat which I know you do eat. There are other potential reasons not to like it. But you can't tell me what they are, and they don't apply to you. Hence, this is an example of you being irrational: the reason why you're here."

"Then why do you call it 'petite meat' and not by its real name? You're irrational too." The two large grey marbles opposite gleamed slightly. The Director set down his knife and fork. "No. You're mistaken. This *is* its name because this is what it's called. Alternatively, if you prefer, garnishing it with this particular label can improve the taste. Improving the taste is rational. Therefore, the label is rational."

"So you've set all this up just to make a point?" John laughed at him, derisively. The Director sat back. "If you don't want me to provide an apprehendable explanation, then I'll leave." He stood up, joining his words in condescension. "Wait," pleaded John. The Director picked up the two plates of food and threw them behind him, before calmly taking his seat again, "As you wish. They became a distraction," he explained, "And you weren't going to eat yours anyway and I'm full."

"Why am I here?" "As I was explaining," resumed the Director General, "you're here on charges of suspected irrationality, with the potential to be impulsively harmful to society. Your trial and sentence are one and the same, and your punishment self-inflicted." "I don't believe you," reacted John, "What about the law computer program and prison overcrowding?"

"Well, indeed the solution to integrate your trial and sentence, to make your current accommodation both prison cell and courtroom, yourself judge, jury, defendant, inmate… and candidate executioner: this was a further efficiency discovered using the law computer program when we set it to handle the problem of death as a sentence; naturally, it also solves one of our original problems you referred to of overcrowding – both within prisons and beyond – of a certain type of undesirable." John's mind grappled with what he'd heard.

Breaking the silence, the Director General continued, "With regard to the law computer program and the problem of prison overcrowding, I admit I wasn't expecting you to remember." An idea struck John. "You have access to my memories, don't you?" he asked, excitedly. "This conversation's not real: it's in my head," he proceeded, recalling the fact from dim recesses, "but my memories are also in here and they *are* real! You can show them all to me and then I'll understand." "No," replied the Director. "Why? Then please at least tell me instead?" "But I just have told you. Are you sure it's truth you want or satisfaction you're after?" "The truth," John told the empty eyes, hopefully. "*The Truth*?" replied the Director. An expression lingered uncharacteristically across the astute features.

"The Truth consists of a web of facts, all interconnected. Since you can't or won't comprehend the key fact as it's been presented to you in relative isolation, perhaps it's best I start with the fundamentals, which can be succinctly built upon to arrive at what is more specifically relevant to your query. In doing so, I'll also have the pleasure to share with you findings of the conceptual analysis program, which will guide us from the general to the specific key fact.

"Why does all of this exist, or indeed why anything? In the beginning, so to speak, there was (or is) an infinite amount of nothingness. 'And why this infinite amount of nothingness?' one might reasonably press with. However, to this question, it can now be more satisfactorily replied, 'And why not? What else would there be?' The relevance: an infinite amount of nothingness is equivalent to or gives rise to something, or indeed anything, and this (this universe, this place, this very experience) is simply one such something.

"The principle of plenitude: everything that can be *is*. Correspondingly, everything that can be experienced *is* experienced. Insofar as the notion of distinct selves, or a plurality of different experiencers (doing said experiencing), is illusory, there is only one experiencer, which can most aptly be called God: indeed being omniscient, omnipotent and omnibenevolent. Its omniscience consists in the infinitude of experience (including yours and mine), and Its omnipotence in freewill. Finally, with no other explanation is there perfect and complete *justice*: for example, otherwise it's unjust for some to be made evil rather than good, or for some to enjoy (or suffer) existence and not others. Hence, God too is omnibenevolent. All real, physical and —"

The Director looked inquisitively at John. "It seems you're sceptical of how this leads to the more specific answers you're after – well it doesn't if you don't engage your attention – or is your stare an incredulous one, intended as a lazy rebuttal?"

"All this from the conceptual analysis program?" replied John. "How can you possibly arrive at all that simply through analysing our concepts? Conceptual analysis is… it's just saying things… in other words… a sort of translation within one language… intralingual translation… isn't it? We ask a philosophical question like 'What is justice?' and the answer is ultimately saying what justice is in other words… within the given language. But it can't tell you… by itself—it's not… "

John glimpsed a perfectly small transparent sphere form fleetingly at the Director's eye, before it collapsed into a line down his cheek. The Director didn't appear to notice.

"Look, I'm really not all that interested in these theories anyway. I still don't see how any of this is relevant to why I'm in the cell?"

"Consider this. During my explanation just now suppose we'd switched places, and you'd experienced giving the explanation and I'd experienced poorly understanding it, and, after the fact, we'd switched back to having these current respective experiences (which comprise the experience of apparent continuity through time, memory, etc.). How do you know, or what would it even mean to say, that this didn't just happen, or happens eternally across all sentience? The distinction between you and me as selves is as correspondingly illusory as that between time and space itself. Naturally, the truth is awesome and terrifying: constituting for Us an infinitude of every experience – however wonderful and ghastly – possib—"

"Why did I wake up one day in a cell with no clue as to how I got there?"

"I think; therefore, there is structure. This we can know with cert—" "Enough!" returned John.

"Quite," replied the Director General. With the single syllable his voice changed to one of alien melancholy. Another man seemed now to sit opposite John, or rather the same man but from a time and place of another world. "We wake up already in the middle of things, John. As to 'Who or what *am* I, after all?' or '*Where* am I?' – such basic, *basic* questions – we all live and die without ever really knowing… tragically, wonderfully, absurdly…" Their separate eyes met, it seemed for the first – and last – time.

The Director restarted, "As I understand it, you'd like to proceed from a more scientific starting point. Is that correct?" John gave no response. Let's begin with an alternative explanation – one final time.

"As a matter of scientific fact, the universe as it is here and now is a rare part of what it is generally. Specifically, it stretches on or out into a future where there is, essentially and forever, nothing: with all planets, stars and people gone. It stretches like this for an eternity—" "*Your* universe may revolve around laws, Director General, but who's to say that *the* Universe does?" John interrupted. The Director seized John's attention while it stood so brazenly out, "*All* of this" – having rapped twice on the table ostentatiously, he slapped John hard in the face – "as it is now, is in fact no more than an infinitesimally small part of a gigantic *nothingness*: ergo *none* of it really exists."

The Director seemed to have finished this time, as he looked at John for a response. John looked up and across the table at the still face opposite. He rubbed his cheek. "There won't be *nothing* though will there?" he replied, "… and that's just a theory involving too many mysterious factors—and even if you have another explanation where everything ends in nothing, or is so, or there's an infinitude of everything or whatever your other theory was…

what about this infinity you're so obsessed with – if we allow that four and five divided by zero are both each infinity, then four and five would be equal, but they're not: two plus two is four, but it is not five. It is infinity which isn't real, not everything else."

"A reply is that it's in precisely that sense that four and five *are* equal: they're both the same in that they're both finite: something, not nothing nor everything… But yes: the problematic or paradoxical concept of infinity raises a good point," replied the Director, pleased, "as regards both theories."

He sat back, apparently enjoying a moment a while waited for, "More importantly, as you've previously recalled from one of our opaque meetings, it's likewise relevant to the technical issues of introducing the death sentence into the law computer program, and so finally brings us back to why you're here…

"It's funny how the subconscious works," the Director mocked, "Obviously, as we've already both agreed, our cozy scene here isn't real and never happened. It can't be a real memory, as within it we've made references to your present circumstances." The dead pupils grew predatory, "But it *feels* real – just as real as your other so-called memories – does it not? What does that tell you, *dummy*?"

As the blank face opposite faded from view, the entire vision just passed remained vivid and John's cheek hurt.

John opened his eyes, as if from blinking, and he knew where he was immediately. His mind felt bloated, and he most wanted to stare blankly up from his pillow at nothing.

However, he couldn't help but notice that the cell lighting was unusual. He slowly brought his view leftwards across the ceiling. The same familiar electric light was there, and it was on. Yet the surrounding glow was different. It was dimmer.

why is the room all dim like this

He looked up at the window to his right. It was gone. The bars proudly stood on show as before, but now before a backdrop of flat metal. It'd been covered up. Directly ahead, on a bleary table, breakfast was ready.

it's morning

A notion spread, like lukewarm glass across John's chest, that life had abandoned him.

The meal on the table was the same dish he'd had for dinner last night: pasta in a thin sauce.

did I miss breakfast, is this lunch

The meal type wrangled with his body clock, but there was now no longer any natural light to adjudicate. Enjoyment of the meal was tainted by the premonition that all future ones would be like it.

After eating, the mellow lighting ordered John back to bed. He wasn't tired. He lay back on the sheets all the same, relaxing into a blank haze. Time passed.

With a click, the glow from the light disappeared. The cell was the blackest it'd ever been. The door opened and John knew other people had entered. They waited at the door. "We're here with your food. Please stay where you are." It was the same voice as before. Already it had become familiar.

John stayed where he was, lying on the bed, looking up into black space. He didn't have the energy to disobey. Invisible sounds came from the end of his bed, at the table. He looked over to the door and saw the elusive shell of a spectre lingering there. The idea of charging for the exit had no life for him. He didn't want confrontation; he'd come to realise he could live without freedom: he just wanted peace. The spectres left and the door was shut. The dull light switched back on, and John was unhappy to espy the same offering of pasta in a thin sauce.

John was pacing the cell. His instincts told him that the meal which he'd just had hadn't been dinner but lunch. Either way, he wasn't ready for sleep. He paused in the dimness to look at the table. Curiosity led him over to crouch down beneath it.

the grenade's still there

He'd wanted to check. He reached out through the hazy light to touch it.

cold metal

His fingertips found their way to the smooth sides of the angular metal protrusion, where the ring pull attached to the main body.

murderer of your wife's husband!

His hand flinched, as if he'd touched an open wound in his own flesh. He shrank away from the table feeling ashamed.

The thinly spread light snapped out once more. Back in bed, though still not tired, John felt the door open. The routine of the spectres repeated itself. When the light switched on, he was relieved to find the food wasn't pasta: it was eggs with watermelon.

but this is breakfast food

He was sure it wasn't breakfast time. Before the lights had come back on, the spectres' timing had supported his instincts that the previous meal was lunch. Now he felt confused.

I'm not drinking the coffee

At the head of his bed, he bent down to pick up the poem. He took it to accompany him at the table with his breakfast (or whatever meal this was).

no, this is dinner not breakfast, I might not have a choice about what food they give me or when but I can decide what meal the food is for me

He became anxious of watermelon juice or egg getting on the poem. He could remember it by heart now. He walked back over to the head of the bed to return the paper to its place there. Having done so, he sat back down at the table with his food before him.

I'll say the poem once before eating

Another world, the tides tweaked a fraction,
The possible swells to a different form,
...
I tread water, feel the depths that plunge down,
Still getting tired refusing to drown.

Gathering up his knife and fork, John began his dinner.

He was soon finished. Having hovered in the background, his craving returned to read the poem with it physically in his hands. He washed his hands at the fountain. He was going to wipe them dry on his loose shirt when he had a better idea. He'd let them dry naturally, whilst pacing the cell, letting his desire build. Only then would he touch the paper.

At last, John's hands were dry. He picked up the paper and laid it carefully on the flat white sheets. Kneeling down, with his elbows pressing into the bedding, he read the poem once out loud.

only once

He had a change of mind.

I've just had the third meal of the day so I'll read it three times

After two more recitals, he removed the poem from its current spot and returned it to its place on the floor, laid by the bed.

The next day, John was keen to implement his new poem-reading routine on breakfast. Sat at the table, he said the poem once before eating. After his meal of cold pasta, he washed his hands at the fountain, before walking up and down the room to let them dry. Completing his task diligently, he then took the poem out. Kneeling down, he laid it on bed, like the night before. However, being the first meal of the day, he read the poem only once. Finally, he moved around to face the head of the bed from behind and returned it to its resting place, laying it in the corner where the bed met the wall on his right.

An idea then emerged before him.

or maybe this time I can lay it on the side at the left of the pillow then after lunch in the centre then after dinner back to where it was on the right, then I can keep track of my meals

The position of the poem would tell him what meal he'd just eaten or was about to eat.

As his pillow greeted the back of his head, John felt content with his system. It wasn't much, but his new behaviour told him he might manage. He was anxious for his new routine to weave firmly into the empty space of time, which currently constituted his life, and so give it a meaningful pattern. With his subtle scheme, he was ready when the next day came. It soon played itself out.

Of special importance, the embroidery of his life-pattern was Amelia's poem. John liked to imagine that through this his wife somehow participated in his current life with him. However, as he read it more, he lost clarity over who wrote it and who it was addressed to.

suppose it was written both by and for myself?

He shuddered.

At first, he had been happy that the spectres were excluded from his life's secret meaning. The ugly pattern they imagined they were imposing had been rejected, and without their even knowing. He liked this. However, his loneliness was persuasive and his pride weak. He wanted others to be a proper part of his routine, and this desire was aware of the albeit-unapproachable spectres.

By now, the light in the cell had snapped off and on a number of times. Presently, it did so once again.

lunchtime

The spectres entered the black cell. The larger one was already at the table, transferring the food. At which point, from the shadowy corner which hid the door, came a clear voice. This other spectre had always been mute before, and John had forgotten that it might be able to talk. "You're going to be released tomorrow." He recognised her voice instantly. It was Lucy.

He leapt up from his bed.

she said I can leave tomorrow!?

"What did you say? I can leave tomorrow?" "Stay where you are," the larger voice of the other spectre by the table told him. It was stern but lacked urgency. From the shadows by the door, Lucy's spectre walked through the black to meet John at the centre of the cell. "You're going to be released tomorrow," she repeated. "Amelia's very excited about it. You should be too." She was close enough to be real now.

Without knowing what was happening, and in chaos, his body had charged into the one in front of it. He'd gripped hold of clothes covering a woman's chest. Behind his clenched hands, shoulder blades had collided into a metal wall. A large hand to his right had caught hold of his throat and pulled him away. A fist cleaved his rib cage, winding him badly, before he was thrown back onto hard flat floor.

John's bright white cell had returned; though it must've been bigger, because in the middle was the large mahogany table of the Law Bureau. He was sat at his usual place, but the places around him were empty. He looked up to the head of the table. His eyes met with the glorious light of the sun, shining down through his cell window. Something else caught his attention: the unassuming bearded man from the Law Bureau, called John, was sat at the head end of the table to the left, just as he had been in the opaque meeting.

John stood up and walked across the white floor against the flow of light. He sat down facing the bearded man opposite, the light from the window shining down through between them onto the mahogany. Yet the bearded man didn't notice him. "Hello?" he asked him. The bearded man straightened up excitedly. Turning a cupped ear to him and leaning out sideways onto his elbow across the polished wood, he replied in a loud whisper, "Hello!?" It was the voice of his neighbour, John.

I knew it!

The man in the meeting and the man in the cell next to his were one and the same.

John leant forwards across the broad table towards his neighbour, whose back was still to the window, "It's me: John – I mean Cameron – John Cameron – your neighbour." His neighbour straightened up and away from his cupped ear, lowering his hand. He was a profile of contempt.

John got up. Seeing there was no space between the head of the table and the window, he hurried along around its other equally broad end. He sat facing his neighbour on the adjacent chair. "Hello?" he repeated, "What's the matter?" His neighbour turned round to the side. His heavy chair had been shifted so that his back was now angled towards the table. He again cupped his ear at him, his arm supported by the chair back. "Yes, yes, I know who *you* are," he said, in tired restraint. He held a small silence. "Traitor!" he spat at the wall opposite.

With confusion, John studied his neighbour's face, "What do you mean? What did I do?" he said, bewildered, to the loathing profile. "'What did I do?'" his neighbour mocked back at him, "You're a traitor! That's what you did. You've the potential for treachery in you." His neighbour looked around his own private space. "And so I'm still stuck in here!" John could certainly relate to his anger.

"But your time-machine idea, it would never have worked," he pleaded. "No, not when you don't follow through on your promises. That's a traitor talking." "But I didn't think it would work," John again pleaded. "It was a good plan – It would've worked. It's absurd but it still would've worked – We could've both escaped. But you lacked faith. You should never have agreed to it if that's how you felt. I should never have trusted you!"

John woke in a jolt with an aching body.

even my dreams are against me

He'd turned in all directions to find where he was deserted. Candidates for answers had long since escaped, forsaking him, with all exits sealed shut. Only their confused hints were perhaps left scattered behind. In the dimness, resounding convictions were drowned in each other's din.

a broken puzzle

This was another conviction, soon to join the noise.

15 ENDS

Standing at the centre of a faded cell, a man leaned simultaneously into surrounding air.

what is a life, not life but a life

A biological definition wouldn't do. Nor would poetry. He felt his had been nothing but a distraction, yet what from, perhaps, was precisely the problem.

life is not an optimisation problem

He addressed the Director.

then what is it?

Asked the Director's floating vacant eyes.

a finite possible set of experiences, its realisation, is that all any life is, all mine is… a subjective possible world… maybe that's enough but why these experiences and not others, and I couldn't have had any others…

it's not necessarily true that I have this thought now

but it must be… are all my thoughts necessarily mine or might I have had others, I couldn't be thinking anything else because then I wouldn't be me, experiencing *being me, and I couldn't* not *be me… and then thoughts are just one part of an intraconnected inner world in turn interconnected with the outer world and inner worlds of others…*

… but how could this mental realm I find myself in interact with the physical, what possible mechanism could there be… but then that's precisely it! interactions and mechanisms, these are physical *concepts, why should they apply between realms… then there's the abstract realm too I suppose, a law isn't something physical you can get your hands on but surely* they *exist, what really exists after all*

maybe it doesn't matter, if it is only the physical then what wonderfully mysterious stuff this physical is to give rise to the other realms

but then how does this trinity all fit together… assuming it does… what is total reality after all…

everything's necessarily as it is, it could never have been any other way because then I wouldn't be me experiencing *this very thought as I* actually *am now*

… destined to do whatever I do now… perhaps my choices determine which world I live in…

perhaps the whole distinction of what's necessary and possible is yet another human myth, invalid… as soon as you start making distinctions the trouble begins…

how has my own life affected the experiences of others, am I guilty, am I good

The possibilities became overwhelming.

who was I in the past, of course my actions have already been done whatever they were, but they were done by me, myself a part of the physical past just as much as anything else, I'm not separate from the Universe and its causality… I have no illusions about my freedom, it doesn't take causal precedence to the chain of events before my birth or natural laws, but then I never felt that it did! I may be subject to the laws but I'm also their embodiment… eternally free to fulfill my destiny… and so that's what I'll do…

of course I will some things, just because I don't will that I will them but that's a silly standard, like not knowing that you know, doesn't mean you know nothing… infinite regresses lurk everywhere it seems… like in Martin's art on the train platform, silly rectangles

Whatever the case, the man didn't want freewill. He just wanted to choose his fate and be done with it.

He had picked a grenade up. Stranded in the remote moment, there was nothing stopping him from jerking its red ring pull free. Gripping the grenade in one hand, his free fingers of the other dangled in the air. A single slight spasm of the muscles and everything would finish forever.

a pointless messy end

He'd be trapped for a few more horrible seconds, then his body would cover the cell's walls or his brain those of his skull.

or alternatively perhaps the grenade was never real, maybe if I pull it they'll finally let me leave, maybe that's the test, it will end curiosity one way or another… at the least the grenade can't be more real than my own life because it contains it… my life ends with me so for me never ends…

but Lucy, she said I'll be released tomorrow, such a pointless tragic end if I kill myself now

The stakes rose swiftly to dizzying heights.

and Amelia… she's looking forward to seeing me again and continuing our life together… but in place of that tomorrow she'd just be shown my lifeless corpse and that would be that… that would be that…

my release… I'll be free! I could do anything… but then what will I do…

I could do anything, on any day, for any year… I could be anyone

I don't have to do what I've always done, I don't even have to be with Amelia, everything's a choice… I'd be free, I am free, whether I admit it or not… though I'm free not to admit it!

He chuckled at the idea. At the same time, such raw freedom inspired awe.

I could be master of myself, at all moments… I'd be the most powerful man in the world

Why he was stood there like this, he didn't know. One vague reason had been to test himself, and triumph, before he left. Now something else was happening.

The being gazed on electric space. Something thin and cold was clasped by the left side. Something else weighed slightly lighter to the right. In a shaded daze, black and red appeared separated by clinical white farther off below. The ring pull caught tight the index finger of Cameron's left hand. In John's right, the weight vanished, as the black metal object, once there, tumbled down through the massy air.

NOW-HERE

Life itself will always be greater than any religion, philosophy or science. It's a constant stream of answers, ending only with you.

Printed in Great Britain
by Amazon